THE CATTLE KILLING

Books by John Edgar Wideman

A GLANCE AWAY

HURRY HOME

THE LYNCHERS

DAMBALLAH

HIDING PLACE

SENT FOR YOU YESTERDAY

BROTHERS AND KEEPERS

REUBEN

FEVER

PHILADELPHIA FIRE

THE COLLECTED STORIES OF
JOHN EDGAR WIDEMAN

FATHERALONG

THE CATTLE KILLING

THE
CATTLE
KILLING

◇ ◇ ◇ ───────────────────────

John Edgar Wideman

HOUGHTON MIFFLIN COMPANY

BOSTON • NEW YORK   1996

For information about this and other Houghton Mifflin
trade and reference books and multimedia products,
visit The Bookstore at Houghton Mifflin on the World Wide
Web at http://www.hmco.com/trade/.

Library of Congress Cataloging-in-Publication Data
Wideman, John Edgar.
    The cattle killing / John Edgar Wideman.
        p.   cm.
    ISBN 0-395-78590-1
    1. Afro-Americans—Pennsylvania—Philadelphia—
History—18th century—Fiction. 2. Afro-American clergy
—Pennsylvania—Philadelphia—Fiction. 3. Africans—
Pennsylvania—Philadelphia—Fiction. 4. Afro-American
families—Fiction. 5. Race relations—Fiction.   I. Title.
PS3573.I26C38   1996   96-19305
813'.54—dc20   CIP

Various texts are "sampled" in this narrative—for instance,
a letter written by Benjamin Rush (August 22, 1793) and
passages from various eighteenth-century diaries and sermons.
I am indebted to these sources and to the historians whose
research has made the documents available. Noël Mostert's
FRONTIERS and Terence Doherty's THE ANATOMICAL
WORKS OF GEORGE STUBBS were also indispensable.

Book design by Robert Overholtzer

Printed in the United States of America

QUM 10 9 8 7 6 5 4 3 2 1

TO JAMILA

who arrived with one of those
tough, beautiful old souls
that's been here
before

PART ONE

Prepare your baggage as though for exile . . .

EZEKIEL 12:3

Setting out for his father's house he leaves everything behind. He even leaves himself behind as he begins the steep climb up Wylie Avenue. He is not himself. Only a character in a story someone else was writing. Why he is so sure of this would be another story, and if he paused to ruminate about other stories he'd never make it up the hill. So he leaves everything behind. The room with the warm bun of her body baking beneath the covers, his room with the black duffle bag unopened on the bed, the little toothpaste-flecked black cosmetics case on the tile counter in the bathroom, leaves the writers' rooms, the rooms of their books, books written, unwritten, promised, betrayed, strayed, broken-hearted books as tangible in the Hotel William Penn's air as somebody's garlic breath sitting next to you at breakfast saying he's always admired your work. Leaves behind the conference, what has occurred so far in the rooms reserved for it, and the fast-fading hopes for it that fast become so many cups of coffee so many drinks and munchies from the bar accumulating on a bill a computer will print out the last morning of your stay and you won't believe it, start to pump yourself up to fiercely deny responsibility and demand an accounting but you don't because you know it would be too painful, recollecting detail by detail the circumstance of each expenditure, you know every item on the bill and more in fact is chargeable to you if you or anybody else bothered to reconstruct how much time you spent here, how you spent it, with whom doing what; thus, rather than live through it all again, you'll sign and leave the bill behind with everything else left behind as you start walking up Wylie Hill, even though you just checked into the hotel a minute ago and the reckoning's just begun.

You step out the hotel door and into another skin. Easy as that. Easy as pie. You are young again in this city. Eye again. Coming up, everybody called you Eye. You hear their voices. The sound of your name brings back the faces of your running buddies. You see Reggie and Scott and Howard and Hamp, but you cannot see the name they say. Is it Eye *or* I *or* Ay *or* Aye *or* Aie.

In this city he is fifteen, fifteen, pimply-faced, skinny and can't dance a lick the really good dancers tease him. He hides behind a red plastic bowl of potato chips on a table in a corner, grease on his fingertips shines in the semidark of somebody's basement waiting for one of the slow, sad songs he listens to at home alone, alone as he ever gets in a house full of brothers and sisters, the record played loud enough to drown out any presence but his own sad self. The record played over and over trancing him to a darkness where he imagines moving smooth-faced and smooth-talking in a groove with the slow grind velvet gimme of the Five Royales or Spaniels or Midnighters or Imperials. His hand in the bowl's slick booty, fingering crumbs too small to pick up except as precious smear of salt and grease he wipes on his lips. A house party maybe it cost a quarter to get in (Bessie Smith said, Humpff — I wouldn't pay twenty-five cents to go in nowhere), maybe not if he gorillaed with a crowd of other youngbloods, lots of bloods, few quarters, shoving in a burst through the door, or maybe he knew the person whose house it was, or maybe this once he just gave up his quarter or dime.

A social. Used to call them socials where you go to rub bellies with fine bitches and end up alone in a corner drowning in a bowl of potato chips. Little things mean a lot, he thinks. Him still with a thing for potato chips, a love-hate weird compulsion and maybe it goes back to those heigh-ho Silver teen days of old. Socials. Security. The potato chip corner he would head for and occupy till he mustered up courage to slip into the tide of dancers on the slowest slow drag love song somebody pulled close enough you don't look at her and she doesn't see you for who you really are. One song over and over and over. Till his mother yells enough now, that's enough please it's coming out my ears now enough enough. Over and over till he knows every note, every word, sings along to himself, wears it like a cloak of invisibility letting him slip into the dance, pull her body tight against his, her gum pop pop in his eardrum, the packed grease of her hair stiff under his chin, the grease of his cheeks, of his fingertips shiny and unnoticed while the song plays and he knows it inch by inch better than it knows itself. She would hear him singing it, the croon and do-wah of it inside his head if he could squeeze her, grind her in there with him. She feels it in the hard knob of him against her thigh. Every beat and dip and swerve of the tune he can depend on to the bittersweet end. Till the dance is finished. While it plays they are somewhere else, the two of them not in somebody's dark, funky basement. Not prisoners with bags over their heads dragged into a courtyard at dawn to be shot.

Fifteen sneaking to a social on the Hill. A bad, black, nappy part of town. Bad people live there. You might get your ass kicked. Or the girls might laugh at you because you couldn't dance the new step *they were dancing on the Hill that week. Chased home. A busted lip. Wounded pride. Forget-me-knots upside your shaved head, and don't let me catch you down here again, chump. Once in a while you hear tales of switchblades and razors, a mean fight and blood everywhere, ambulances, cops. A long nasty scar on someone's throat. That's why you had to sneak to the Hill. Why your mother would die if she knew. You lie and make a beeline just where you know better than to go. Promise me you won't go down there. I promise. Promise. Truth's not in you, is it, boy. I know exactly where you've been.*

Aw, Mom. Hill ain't no worse than noplace else.

Fifteen. Last night on the hill at whose foot the William Penn Hotel and the rest of downtown gleam, last night a black boy fifteen shot in the face and dying. Another black boy a year younger already dead from bullets in the chest. At a party. Perhaps in the basement of one of the row houses where they had those fifteen-cent, twenty-five-cent socials. Girls shrieking, gunshots like virtual reality leaping from the hip-hop soundtrack of one of the tunes they dance to now. Over and over again. The beat shaking the walls, the floorboards. People surging back and forth. Fire in the hole. Fire in the hole. A stampede to the door — pop pop — then back into the darkness of the shotgun row house. Gun booms inside or outside, you can't tell. But it's large, large. Inches from your ear. You're humped up to whoever's next to you in the dark, smashed together, driven by whoever's mixing and scratching and sampling this nightmare thumping around your head. Feet one way, arms another, your hips bumped and smacked and slammed you might be upside down in the funky house or sprawled on the sidewalk. Bang. Bang. Somebody's dead. It might be you in one of those trifling juke-joint-for-a-night shacks up on the hill you climb toward where your father lives alone.

Shoot. Chute. Black boys shoot each other. Murder themselves. Shoot. Chute. Panicked cattle funneled down the killing chute, nose pressed in the drippy ass of the one ahead. Shitting and pissing all over themselves because finally, too late, they understand. Understand whose skull is split by the ax at the end of the tunnel.

The cattle are the people. The people are the cattle.

Love song once. Then a dirge. The image haunts him. Xhosa killing their cattle, killing themselves, a world coming apart. A brave, elegant African people who had resisted European invaders until an evil prophecy convinced them to kill their cattle, butcher the animals that fleshed the Xhosa's intricate dreaming of themselves.

Xhosa country a slaughterhouse. First the swollen carcasses of cattle everywhere. Then the starving people, dreamless and broken, dying as their cattle had died, exiled from the ark of safety that had been home and culture and heritage. Too many dead to bury. Survivors learn to avoid corpses, tip around them, ignore the smell. Too weak to chase off hyenas, jackals, clouds of vultures squabbling, feasting. The Xhosa homeless, destitute, sick, begging food from settlers, skulking in the shadows, ghosts roaming the bush at the edges of European towns, a proud people become like the worthless dogs they always had been in the whites' eyes.

He wanted every word of his new book to be a warning, to be saturated with the image of a devastated landscape. To be hurt by it as he'd been hurt. Wasn't the stench of that ravaged countryside burning his eyes, his nostrils as he trudged up Wylie Hill. His book beginning and ending here. The Xhosa, seduced by false prophecy, false promises, turning away from themselves, trying to become something else, something they could never be. Killing their cattle, destroying themselves, dooming their ancient way of life. Deadly prophecy in the air again. The people desperate again, listening again.

Eye. Why are you called Eye. Eye short for something else some-one named you. Who named you Isaiah. What could they have been thinking of. Not this story. Not this place. Not this book all the stories bound together might equal if one of the narratologists at the conference decides you're attempting something like Sherwood An-derson for Ohio or Faulkner for Mississippi or something even more exotic-sounding and harder to pronounce than Yoknapatawpha. Not quite stories. True and not true (check out the facts, dates, murders). Not exactly a novel. Hybrid like this old new ground under your feet as they pound up Wylie.

You are Eye because you grew up in this city. And fifty years later you've returned once more as you always do and your mother and father sister brothers aunts uncles cousins nieces nephews still live here and remember you and remember what they named you and call you by that name. So why not. In a half a century you've invented nothing better or more prophetic than Eye. Plus you're used to it. The sound over and over while you slouch in a dark corner almost master of the art of disappearing except the shine of your greasy lips and greasy fingertips keeps giving you away. Finger-tips the emery board you pilfer from your mom's purse can't pare without sounding like a buzz saw even the saddest song won't drown out.

Later today in the Riverboat Room you'll read to the assembled conferees from the book under your arm. It's there like a splint or superglue keeping one arm sealed, broken wing, to your side. This is the new book, Daddy. Work in progress. Not exactly finished yet but close, close, I hope. It's been a long time coming. Fresh off the press. I picked it up yesterday afternoon from Beth, the woman who does my typing. Haven't even proofread the copy yet. A book nearly finished now, Daddy, so it's like this city, like a tomb, all the books it might have been, could or should have been, buried in its pages. I can't read what's here without mourning what's lost. But I want to share it with you. I've never read to you. Not in fifty years. I mean you've been in an audience and listened or not listened along with everybody else. I mean never just the two of us. Up close and personal. Me reading to you, Dad. A first.

I go up Wylie Avenue to my father's house. Walking the steep slope's like climbing a ladder. After ten minutes the city shrinks below me. Crossing its girdle of broad streets, avenues and expressway ramps had been as treacherous as fording a stream rock by slippery rock, impossible if traffic's running high and fast. In the maze of asphalt arteries it's hard to tell the direction from which cars will come at you. A nagging fear of being blind-sided. Rear-ended. No signs or lights for a pedestrian's use because nobody's supposed to be walking where cars flash suddenly into view around corners, down ramps, four lanes funneling into one or splitting and each tributary curves or darts somewhere no driver expects to see a person on foot picking his way over dividers, scrambling onto a narrow ledge of curb, occupying the dead still center that is only an imaginary space formed by lanes converging and crisscrossing.

> You have placed your trust in maps, ships, captains. That is a good form of trust, but it does not of itself lead to salvation. I have heard that bodies have been dismembered in Bruges to discover what lies within a human being. In Arras we have done the same, but to a different end. We were moved by hunger, not curiosity. And it is for that reason that we know a hundred times more about man!

He's decided on this epigraph from the book uncannily similar in conception and execution to his, A Mass for Arras. By a Polish writer, Andrzej Szczypiorski, one of those names bristling with unfamiliar clusters of vowel and consonant, daring you to attempt pronouncing it. A Mass for Arras. The title rhymes in English. In Polish?

In this city of hills and bridges and clannish ethnic neighborhoods where Eye grew up, all the tribes of Eastern Europe claimed turf. He remembers their halls and social clubs, churches and posters bearing the long strange names — Lithuanian Czechoslovakian Armenian Ukrainian Yugoslavian Macedonian. Words chiseled in different alphabets, words with odd combinations of letters discouraging him from trying to say the sounds they might represent. Nobody he knew said the words either. Wherever they came from, whatever they called themselves or inscribed on their buildings or banners, these thick, funny-talking white people, old women in headscarves and long black dresses, men in tacky clothes nobody would wear unless they didn't know any better, were hunkies — as in short for Hungarians maybe or maybe because they were heavy-limbed, earth-hugging, silent hunks of people, broad-browed, thick-handed, wide-cheekboned, broad-beamed, deep-eyes-always-elsewhere people. Hunkies he saw again, an unexpected flood of Pittsburgh memories in the black faces of rural South African women decades later carrying a man who'd been shot by the blue-butt instant cops after a rally in Crossroads.

On his right, below him now, the Civic Arena with its already obsolete version of space-age retracting roof, the vast acres of parking lot that had once been Italian, then Jewish, then a black neighborhood, the Lower Hill a kind of Ellis Island ghetto where the latest off the boat settled first, stuck in a slum of tenements and boarding houses until they learned the trick of moving out, disappearing into other quarters of the town. Was he in high school when the Lower Hill was razed to make way for the Civic Arena and its parking lots, for a futile renaissance and remodeling and cleansing of urban space.

Had Eye really been fifteen when all those houses on the Hill torn down, the black people who lived in them chased. And still running, emigrants with nowhere else to go. Then or now. Was Eye fifteen then. Is he always fifteen plus or minus fifteen, in the story I tote up the hill to my father's house. An indeterminate, approximate age stripped of specific features, a hunky age, nigger age, because who needs to remember the goofy-sounding names, the faraway places where all these tribes, black or white, once lived. Who cares what they once called themselves. Who cares if they still do.

A generic kid, peeking like Kilroy over the edge of coming of age, unformed, inarticulate for the most part, except for what he does with his body playing sports, what he'd dance if he could, what he sings silently inside his own head accompanying music in which he hears voices speaking to him, for him, about him, who he actually is, what he feels, the precious loves and lessons and exploits he must listen to over and over until he gets them just right. Except for these exceptions Eye speaks little about himself so words can be put in his mouth, his dreams, and claim to be him. Eye is a convenience, a sort of in-person once-upon-a-time convenience when I write his name. Eye, any kid, your kid, you, me, mine, one or both of the boys blown away at the party last night up on the hill where my father's high-rise apartment building looms, bull neck with no head.

On the phone about a month ago my Aunt K, my father's sister who lives in the same public housing senior citizens' complex where my father resides, called to say my father was very sick. A flu had been smacking people down, down for weeks at a time, an especially dangerous and occasionally fatal flu when it attacked the very young and old. To make things worse she said the drowse of flu, the grogginess induced by over-the-counter drugs with which he treated himself, had caused my father to drift off to sleep after he'd started running a bath. Whole apartment flooded. A maintenance guy had used one of those industrial vacs to suck up most of the water, but the damp carpeting still squishes underfoot in places, sets a permanent chill in the air. It's this cold, stale swamp I march toward. My dad trapped in it.

If he could, he'd set his eighteenth-century boy walking in streets as real as these Hill streets. But he didn't know those other streets, quiet now two hundred years. Not quiet really. For his young African man streets alive with wheelbarrows and carts, the iron-rimmed wheels of wooden wagons, men on horseback, in chariots, chaises, carriages and coaches clattering against cobblestones, the echoing cries of oystermen, farmers vending produce, loud gossip around the water pumps, dogs and livestock, chickens in baskets, church bells, a fiddle in a tavern, auctioneers in the slave market bid 'em in, bid 'em in, gunshot crack of a whip or a huge oak cask rolling down a narrow alleyway, laborers chanting to keep time for the lifting, the sawing, hammering, street sounds alive because the young African man strides full of life among them.

He hears the pulse but cannot name it. Only the young man could say its proper names. The many names it needed to be real. He was not the African youngster, never was, never would be, so he could not feel the sleeve of air that had enclosed him, nor hear the sounds piercing it, stitching it together so it would be worn like a comfortable garment, forgotten once donned, yet there, doing the work it should, intimate as a second skin.

What he shared with the eighteenth-century African boy whose story he wanted to tell, the thing he would try to write, the thing that must replace names only the boy could give to what it felt like to be moving through clangorous streets, dead for two hundred years, what he could construct, would be testimony witnessing what surrounds them both this very moment, an encompassing silence forgetting them both, silence untouched by their passing, by the countless passings of so many others like them, a world distant and abiding and memoryless. The terror of its forgetfulness, its utter lack of concern would be unbearable unless he imagined something else, someone else, passing like him, and their many passages though each a shadow also the substance these streets, these downtown traffic sounds shape themselves around, moment to moment, a life beginning, ending before the stillness, even as stillness reigns.

The boy shot dead on the hill last night. His ancient African lad meeting his brethren as he thinks the meeting, as he unleashes himself from this time, this moment beginning the climb to his father. What is the name of the space they occupy now. All of them. The black boy always fifteen, the two boys freshly dying, the long-gone African, his father.

Was it a lie, a coverup to say they've all looked into the same sky, walked the same earth and thus share a world, a condition. Even so, given the benefit of the doubt, what kind of world is it. Why is it not weeping for everything lost. And why is he afraid of dying. And who is he anyway, interchangeable with these others, porous, them running through him, him leaking, bleeding into them, in the fiction he's trying to write. He glances back at the many-storied hotel, higher towers of steel and glass framing it, dwarfing it. The snarl of traffic he'd negotiated minutes ago at the foot of the hill. If it's all gone tomorrow. If yesterday none of it sprawled there, if someone, traders in a canoe, Frenchmen, a Negro slave, an Iroquois guide, is drifting down a green river, quiet, exhausted, the Europeans overwhelmed suddenly by the land's sheer immensity, forests stretching league after league beyond the riverbanks, the white sky pregnant with unpredictable weather, swarms of voracious insects and birds and beasts patiently waiting to feed on intruders no matter how many of the creatures the men in the canoe shoot and skin and squash and eat, men losing faith in their gods, their maps, reneging on the promise they'd pledged to themselves to endure, hold on no matter what until the bend in the river, the fabled golden junction of three great westward-flowing waterways where the tales say you will find yourself if you endure the journey. No city there when they reach the three rivers' magical convergence. When they arrive, will they dream towers of steel and glass rising from the wilderness. This city, this dream. Or another. And if they do and die dreaming and then you find yourself here, where they once were and the kids are here in those savaged row houses bleeding where you hid when you were fifteen, plus or minus, so what.

He would read to his father. Or offer to read. His father not an easy man. He'd read from the new manuscript if his father in bedroom slippers, hunched on the couch, swaddled in blankets against the chill, was willing to listen. And will that listening, if it happens, be part of the story, the beginning of what he reads.

Certain passionate African spirits — kin to the ogbanji who hide in a bewitched woman's womb, dooming her infants one after another to an early death unless the curse is lifted — are so strong and willful they refuse to die. They are not gods but achieve a kind of immortality through serial inhabitation of mortal bodies, passing from one to another, using them up, discarding them, finding a new host. Occasionally, as one of these powerful spirits roams the earth, bodiless, seeking a new home, an unlucky soul will encounter the spirit, fall in love with it, follow the spirit forever, finding it, losing it in the dance of the spirit's trail through other people's lives. ◇ ◇ ◇

During the night the lake has disappeared. Down the slope, through the trees where the lake should be, he sees only a dense white curtain of mist.

The curtain's top is dissolving. White smoke straggles into the pale sky, forming a scattering of small clouds. Sunlight seeping over the rise behind him dyes these puffs of mist soft shades of orange and pink. When he gazes higher, the sky surprises him. A blue ceiling many lifetimes distant. Layer after transparent layer of blue, giving way to more blue, color the lake might turn later in the day, if the lake's still there behind the floating bank of mist.

What color was the water now. Was it there now, gray now, the gray of clinging sleep he rubs from his eyes.

The air is clearing. More blue and deeper as light spreads enormously across the sky. Staring into the snowy mist he listens for forest sounds, waits for them while he thinks words for what the sounds will be. All the words he knows not enough to name the unheard sounds in this shifting place between waking and sleep, sleep and waking.

Wind from the west pushing the mist. A chill wind that had hurdled over the mountains while he slept. He'd been lucky. This kind of wind could bring the season's first snows. The hollow he'd curled into, the roof of pine boughs, would have been scant protection against the buckets and buckets of snow these first storms merrily dump.

In the stripped woods dawn is light here and there on certain trees, here and there. Light silently changing everything. Night becomes morning, morning peels the gray skin from trunks and branches, but if he kept his eyes shut, he wouldn't know what changes dawn had wrought until he opened them. Light silent as time this morning. Other mornings light crashed down around him like summer cloudbursts pounding the thick foliage these bare woods wear in that season.

He fears the light. A wet rag wiping a filthy window. You see out now, now anyone can see in. Some new thing suddenly appears, yet it bears the silent weight of memory. Sleeping a long, deep sleep, but now. Now. Now you must face what has come in the night and lain down beside you. Why are you afraid to turn and look.

He waits, holding his breath while the house that is the world remembers its shape, erects itself again, all the stone and brick and wood piling up without a sound. He goes to sleep alone in an empty place and next morning the cities of his past, the cities of his future, are spread around him. People step over him, around him, through him, always on their way somewhere else. They wear strange shoes, unimaginable shoes, so he understands immediately he is not dreaming, he is awake in a familiar town filled with nameless faces. People wearing shoes cobbled by devils.

People who do not speak to him. Their language unintelligible as the caw-cawing of crows. Yet their voices inflict messages, messages exact as the arrow that will pierce his hand when the old man's ax splinters.

Like an echo of his thought of them, crows shatter the silence. He searches the treetops but can't find the birds. They bicker. Squawks of pain and outrage. Something raw and grating forced down their throats, gagging them. One hobbles into view, bulky black body precariously balanced on twig legs. It hops off the ground. Flight a stuttering fall till the crow's hooked by an invisible line and yanked away. More black silhouettes glide overhead, shuttles through the stark loom of trees.

Light shimmers, smokes, light gouges bark from the trees. Light quakes and shivers, things shy from its glare. Light deceives. A meaningless play upon surfaces, a glint on the blade of his ax, the moon's bright face, late-afternoon dazzle of a million polished coins afloat on the lake, fool's gold that burns and doesn't sink until a gust of wind sweeps away the disguise.

Light struck dumb since the moment it witnessed sin.

Only fire, the crackle and roar of flame, restores what God sundered when He separated light and darkness, tore the tongue from one, hid truth in the other.

Certain trunks, certain limbs beset by light, speckle the woods this morning. Why are some chosen and others not to bear the light. He waits for an answer. Hears only squabbling birds he can't see.

This dawn painted limb by limb, spot by spot on the soft earth, a bath of errors he lowers himself into, sinking again, naked again. Seduced again.

A trial by ordeal. God applies light's weight, its silence. Will I break. Will the spinning earth rise up again and bloody my face. A whirl of fiery sunspots around my head. All colors heated to a white blur. He recalls a hot wind toppling him, stranding him on his back. Upside down, pitching side to side, helpless and mute as a turtle.

The preacher, crow black in his long coat, had said, Men are blinded by the light. Seduced by appearances. Mistake husk for core. Settle for what can be seen. Stake their immortal souls upon appearances. The word *appearances* like some worrisome morsel at last dislodged from a crevice between the exhorter's yellow teeth, spit at the crowd of curious passersby.

This show — the preacher's arms described an arc from horizon to horizon, an arc embracing all four corners of the earth, a lid sealing beneath itself what men take as solid and plant their feet upon — this, all this, is not real. Yet you steadfastly believe it is. You're taken in. You think you see but you don't. The mountains, the marble-pillared houses of government, have no more substance than taunts and whispering and stares of the devil's agents sent to plague you. Phantoms. Ignore them and they have no power over you. Learn to look inside yourselves. Feed the light. If God's taper does not burn brightly in your chest, you're blind as the worm groping between your thighs.

He remembers a shopkeeper he'd caught staring at him. Above the bloody apron tied high as a bib under his chin, the man's features had turned inside out, a steaming pie of gore suddenly exposed. The mask the man manages to pull over his face when he turns to deal with a customer whose skin is not white does not disguise the brutal stewing. It hovers between them. A horror they cannot speak of, hanging plainly as the skinned, decapitated animals on hooks from walls and ceiling beams of the butcher shop. It renders both of them false-tongued as the light. The butcher's face conforming to some lie or another, him sullen or stupid or mute as the white butcher assumed a black man entering his shop must be.

The light, everywhere now. Anyone who cares to look can see the body of a man lying on the ground, a man who's gathered pine spill like some creature of the forest to nest himself.

He thanks God for a new day, for the strength to rise, for breath in his body preserved through the night. He stretches his stiff limbs, shivers as he remembers how cold he'd been during the night, how cold he will remain always, a chill deep within, even if he were tied to a stake and burned as a witch.

He listens to the forest, the sounds you don't hear until you stop listening to yourself. Then you hear yourself. Your name an unspoken presence given shape and substance by the noises patterned around you.

The old man watches him through the window. The slot in the cabin wall is an eye, shutter hooked open above it a lid, the round, dark head the eye's pupil, unmoving in the fainter darkness framed within the opening. A presence inside the cabin more felt than seen. Or rather, once seen, impossible to ignore, there always whether you see it or not each time your eyes stray from the task at hand. You cannot help yourself. You chop. Logs split. You check the window again and again. Is the man still there, staring. You can't be certain. He may be asleep, even dead for all you know, for all you can tell from his featureless silhouette.

With a will of their own your eyes rise stupidly, hopefully to the bait, as if you might prove something you couldn't prove before. Confirm him there in the window, as if the weight of his watching eyes did not sit already, undeniable as a bone in your throat.

Each log split is dawn bursting, sudden and naked. What was

enfolded inside, secured layer by layer, year by year with rings of growing wood, explodes in yellow splinters. His wrists then his shoulders register the pain of the wood, the impact of the falling ax ricocheting back at him, rippling lines of force almost visible, riding across the skin of air.

The ax handle is unsound. In his fists a faint warning, a vibration lasting half a measure longer than it should after the blade bites through a log's clenched heart. He knew it as soon as he lifted the ax from its rigging of cobwebs beside the old man's fireplace. Before he hallooed, before he knocked at this cabin door, he knew that what he would encounter was better left alone. Go further, he'd said to himself. Ignore this desolate hut in its desolate clearing. You'll find a more likely place ahead. Trudge on. Forget the growing emptiness in your belly, the dull ache in your African feet already this morning.

The farm had appeared deserted. A picture of gloomy ruin in the morning mist. Broken fences, an empty lean-to whose roof had collapsed. Weeds and brush thick in spaces that might once have been garden, yard, pasture. He hallooed not because he expected an answer but to alert the ghosts inside the cabin, give them a chance to flee so when he pushed open the door, their cold, spidery breath would not crawl across his face. If the ghosts paid no mind to his voice, if they hunkered down to abuse him for trespassing, his calling out might at least stir up the dogs that were a deadly hazard of these backcountry dwellings. The barking, snapping, leaping kind preferable to silent ones that skulked out of sight, patiently stalking him.

Whether or not the sound of his voice raised dogs, ghosts or someone to answer the door, he'd shouted into the stillness to hear himself shout. To break the pall of silence, rouse himself from the dead.

Long before he noticed the slot of window, a dark shape in one corner, he'd sensed someone observing his approach. Sure the house was empty and sure eyes tracked him as he entered the clearing. The weight of another, real or imagined, seen or unseen, had challenged him. Eyes looking past him, through him, him the stranger ignored, wished away. Did he need someone else's eyes to make him real. Would he disappear if the eyes denied him. Like mist the sun was chasing, would he fade into the dark wall of trees from which he'd emerged.

Before he opened the door, he hallooed twice more at the threshold, mossy green stumps embedded like paving stones in the ground.

A man wrapped in a blanket or cloak or animal skin that draped his body and merged with shadows pooled on the floor was propped against the slot in the far wall. Either he was a very short man standing or an ordinary-size one sitting. Except to blink and fling up one hand to fend off the brightness flooding the open door, he showed no sign of life.

Begging your pardon, good sir. Good day, sir. Might you have work for an honest, hungry Christian. A willing, able pilgrim who begs only a crust of bread for his labor.

Standing in the mouth of this black cave, a sack slung over his shoulder containing all he owned in the world, he could hear light crackling at his back, an inferno coldly consuming him.

When the man didn't answer, he felt small, then awkwardly large, a boy who'd accidentally scuffed his foot against an anthill, terrorizing hordes of startled insects.

Perhaps the old man's deaf, or one of the stubborn, clumsy-tongued lowlanders from across the sea who scorned English.

One swift glance around the cabin's interior enough to answer his own question. No food here. Endless work to get after outside and inside but no food to spare for a passing stranger. A dying farm. In a day, a few hours, this poor soul robed in rags to his chin would be dead too. The chill of death, its stink and silence, ruled here already. He'd pushed open the door of a tomb.

He inches backward. Anxious to escape without disturbing the scene further.

Are you the devil.

Surely not, good sir.

The voice from the grave stopped him in his tracks. He shivers. Measures ashes heaped like gray, drifted snow in the fireplace.

Had the man actually spoken. He wasn't certain now. Yet the echo of some abrupt exchange haunted the silence. A footprint discovered on an island where you are marooned. Suddenly you are less alone and more alone. On his missions to save souls, journeying deep into the backcountry, encountering no other human being for days, sometimes when he'd stop to rest, voices would descend from the air above his head, a host of visitors, a halo of voices floating in exactly this familiar, churning silence.

Black Satan.

I assure you sir, he assures himself, I am no devil. I serve the Good Lord. Preach the truth of His word to all souls willing to listen. With His light in your bosom, sir, you need not fear Satan. Nor any man.

You come too late for her, devil.

He follows the man's eyes to a narrow slab of logs lashed together like a raft. It could have served as a bed. A carcass-shaped mass that could have been a mattress and bedding slumps over one corner. Bed or boat or sled, it throws a shadow of stink that fills the interior. He winces, turns away.

Leave me in peace, black devil.

You have nothing to fear from me. I am a humble servant of God. A witness to His goodness and glory. Let me help you, sir. I'll build a fire. Chop wood for your hearth. And if it please you, sir, pray with you before I take my leave.

An ax leans against the soot-stained stones of the fireplace. One step and it's in his hand. Three more long strides would thrust him through the far wall.

When he turns again toward the man, he finds him cowering against the wall, his face contorted in fear, even whiter now caught full in the window's sparse light.

He doesn't understand the man's terror till he follows his stare to the dangling ax. Ax and face two pale eyes fixed on each other in the darkness.

Mercy. Mercy, please.

The backswing of the ax seems to lift him off the ground. Weightless an instant, unhinged from the consequences of its fall, till the shudder of his weight returns when the blade strikes home. A second freedom then. The soft melt of meeting no resistance. Log splits, two pieces drop separate to the earth.

Flecks of blood on the new page the ax has opened. He glances up at the window. Does he need someone to tell him what's happened. Was there a witness. Who. Where. Why was the split log sprinkled with black drops of blood.

He lets the ax slide from his fingers, hops backward as it dances with a life of its own from one chunk of wood to another. Lodged in the webbing between thumb and first finger, a splinter from the shattered ax handle has skewered his hand. No pain yet. Only silent blood dripping.

He's done something stupid, yes. Perhaps if he tells it right, he won't seem a complete fool. The accident should never have occurred. Ax handle obviously dangerous. I'm fortunate I wasn't injured more severely. Should have known better. The handle had brayed a warning with each blow. He's amazed how calmly he's reciting the story of the wound to himself. He spreads the fingers of his injured hand, turns it this way and that to determine the extent of the damage, to remember the best way to describe it later.

An arrow sticks in his flesh. He holds his hand up for the old man at the window to see.

Searing pain kicks in. He squeezes his eyes shut. The hand, the curious wound, belong to him, after all. He should have yanked out the splinter in the blessed second of numbness. Does the man in the window nod gravely, agreeing, disappointed in him again. Pain a throbbing pulse now. The needle of wood will break off inside his flesh if he's not careful.

He stares at his good hand till it stops shaking. Grips the thicker end of the splinter between thumb and first finger. Pulls.

Look. See how small and harmless it is now.

Over too quickly. For a moment his hand had appeared enormous, the trespass of the splinter a deadly threat. He wanted to examine the strangeness of it all once more. Take his time. Rotate the hand again, appraise it from various angles. His curled fingers an image of Christ's agony. Petals of a flower slowly opening to expose the nail driven through his palm.

The splinter had slid out smoothly. Disappointingly small. No shreds of torn meat, a few more drops of blood. Easier to remove than the old man's prying eyes.

The wound wasn't much, but he must work, when there is work, with his hands. Healing will be slow, soreness something he'll carry away with him from this wretched place. He can hear the man chiding him for chopping wood with a bad ax, wasting tinder to build a fire for a ghost, almost lopping off a foot when he dropped the ax.

He snaps the splinter in two, tosses it away. The sting in his hand more humiliation than pain, like the bite of the driver's switch across his backside when he was herded with the other black boys, away from foolishness, back to their chores.

Inside the cabin again, he watches a spectral part of himself separate from his body, himself split in two so swiftly and cleanly he feels no pain, only curiosity while the second self snatches the old white man's feet, jerks him so hard he flies out from under the blanket, kicking, twisting, tearing out loose hunks of flesh as he's dragged corkscrewing from the wound. Who's screaming. Or is it crows with knives in their beaks murdering the silence that arches like a pewter roof over his head. *Are you the devil.*

I'm sorry, sir. Your ax. It's broken, sir. The handle shattered as I chopped wood for your hearth.

The man ignores him. His mouth gapes. A black pit in his face.

I arrange a layer of kindling atop the ashes, build a bunker of logs. The old man remains silent, unmoving, while I make numerous trips out and back for wood. I scrape sparks from a flintstone. Coax smoke, then flame from a mound of dried grass. Fire catches. Shivers in the dark, icy corners of the room.

Wood squeals, old wood buckled and warped, groaning as I seal the cabin door in its frame. I'm tempted to peek inside one last time, think better of it. Might as well address a block of stone. My work finished here. Such as it is.

I implored — nay, begged — the poor man to pray with me. He answered not. Saint or sinner I knew not. I left him as I found him, wrapped in his rags, his head slumped against the wall, his unblinking eye holding the fire's reflection.

May God have mercy on your soul, I said to the holes that were his eyes, ears, the hole of his mouth.

This is his ax.

The very ax. Swaddled in its bandages, yes it is. You may rest assured he had no more use for it. A pitiful tool it is besides. I removed nothing else from the hovel. But I attach no virtue to my forbearance, if forbearance it was, since naught else in the hut would tempt a thief, let alone tempt one such as I, who though poor claimed to be an honest, God-fearing man.

I carried away the ax because by my own peculiar reckoning I believed I held an interest in it.

It had injured me, you see. Tasted my blood. It owed me. Or perhaps I felt I had earned it. A peculiar reckoning, I grant you. The business does not sit easily in my mind. Not yet, after the passage of many years. There's thievery in it. And pagan superstition. And self-deception, doubtless. Vanity too. You can tell, can't you, my dear friend, I'm also a bit proud of my trophy. Some small revenge exacted, though for precisely what, I hesitate to say.

I've shored up the handle, as you can see, and kept the ax close by me since. It hurt me once. Perhaps its destiny is to wound me again. But I ramble. Spin too much meaning from a simple tale. I found a dying man. I stole his ax.

You're not free of him yet.

Free of *it*, you mean. Once I dreamed a burning coal leapt from the fire I'd started. In less time than it takes to tell, flames had reduced the cabin to cinders. The forest reclaimed the clearing, springing up as I gazed in amazement. Grass, brush, towering trees, instantly restored. No trace of the dwelling. Except in the story I knew I was bound to tell.

Bound.

As I'm bound to the ax.

The ax in its bindings you've bound round the handle.

You tease me.

No. I'm thanking you for your story. But I think you must leave now. Is your story finished.

At your pleasure, dear lady. Finished for tonight.

Is there more, then. Are you teasing me, now.

No, no. My tales are poor, untidy things. No beginnings nor ends. Orphan tales whose sole virtue is you listen. Goodnight. May your dreams be pleasant.

Pleasant or unpleasant, my dreams fly away when I awaken. Would that my demons behaved so. The demons drawn up around my bed each morning, waiting to begin their feast. They never leave me. Bound to me as your crippled ax is bound to you.

One morning you'll open your eyes and everything will have changed. God's best blessing and worst curse upon us. Change, always change.

Not you, my dear friend. You must never change. Tell me you will return tomorrow. And the morrow, and the morrow.

Yes. Of course. As long as there's breath in this body.

Goodnight, then. Till tomorrow.

Till tomorrow. Goodnight.

Goodnight.

Goodnight.

He blows out the candle, climbs down the ladder, and passes through the room where anxious faces are full of questions. He raises a finger to his lips. He had warned them the cure might take weeks. Explained he must effect the cure his way. No interference, no questions. They let him pass. He joins the animals sleeping in the barn. Tiptoes past their separate versions of sleep, of dream, distinct from one another as wing from hoof, beak from snout.

The scent of her holds a short while, in his nostrils, on the hand that had rested a moment on her shoulder after he tugged up the quilt. Her warmth too, retained in his thighs which had settled on the edge of the bed where she'd been lying before he came to her and she had rolled over and sat up to make room for his story. The many stinks of the animals, their stirrings and pungent dreams, the frigid night air cresting each chink in the barn's plank wall, quickly turned what lingered from his hour with her into memory. But not immediately, not depriving him of her till his senses had tasted her reality here, in this place where he spent his nights, nights not bearable unless he knew he could bring her with him, here, as well as go to her sickbed in the loft for the hour they alloted him each evening.

What would be unbearable was *never*. Living where she could *never* come. The length of her visits might shrink to a heartbeat's duration, each one precarious as a heartbeat, but that would still be infinitely preferable to never. He'd bring what he could of her back with him each night to the barn, and no matter how minuscule the something was, it defeated *never*. He could live for it. Had lost any desire to live without it.

In the noisy sleep of the animals captive in the barn were chases and fields and skies and forests. In their upside-down night world he'd learned to share, the animals wandered freely, eating, flying, making love. They shat and their fecund sleep droppings fertilized that nether world. From the black sea of their soil grew another world, sooner or later righting itself as a wooded shoreline rights itself climbing out of still water along its banks. In their sleep, their dreams, he would sow what he'd carried away of her. Her smell. Her heat. She'd be free to grow stronger, new, till she was ready to emerge from the mirror of the water, clamber naked onshore, changed as seasons and dreams changed the land.

I cannot say I was not forewarned. Even if I hadn't talked with my African brethren whose wealthy masters were amongst the first to flee the stricken city, the plain evidence of my own eyes would have revealed the magnitude of the emergency — heavy traffic of wagons, carts, carriages on the main road, abandoned possessions boxed and bundled alongside it, the country homes of prosperous city merchants occupied out of season, temporary shelters sprawling in the fields, families, gangs, packs, whole columns of poor folk wandering aimlessly in the countryside, sleeping in the open wherever they dropped exhausted at night, the dead and dying who'd crawled off the main thoroughfare to expire in the bush.

A plague was ravaging the city. Many of the able-bodied, and those who believed themselves able-bodied till the fever snatched them back into its deadly embrace, were deserting the great city my call to save souls had brought me near.

I can say the word *plague* to you and you shudder as I shuddered hearing it before I had lived through a plague. Now the word for me is merely a word. A vaguely familiar acquaintance recalled from the distant past. Attached to it are memories, melancholy associations from a time before I'd lived through horrors the word *plague* attempts to name. An innocent period when the word was unfleshed, so to speak, before it became so many things, too many things, and lost its power to instill terror, so dwarfed were my expectations by the crushing force of the plague itself. *Plague* almost a tame word now. It invokes a nostalgia for a time when I knew it only as a word. It does not, cannot convey the unspeakable experiences that altered my understanding of the life we lead on this earth.

I employ the word *plague* and wince, avert my eye before I peer through the door the word opens. So insufficient. Even as I observe the word set its chill on you. I pray you will never live in a city beset by plague, and pray that if you must, the worst images of it you can conjure now will be the worst that ever befall you. Because there is worse. Much worse than the worst you can imagine. Far more, far worse.

Plague. A plague of fever was destroying the city. It brought the city to me. To the sparsely populated hinterland where I preached God's word. And it changed me. A second conversion of my spirit, no less affecting than discovering God's light.

My elder brother and I had purchased our mother's freedom, then our own. Soon afterward the God she adored chose to take my blessed mother to His side, and within a year I also lost my brother, who had shipped aboard a vessel bound for the Cape of Good Hope and never returned. Our little household was no more. Full of grief, alone, I despaired of ever finding again the joy and comfort we'd shared in our humble circle of love. In the midst of this darkness I discovered an inner light I believed no earthly trouble nor torment could extinguish.

I heard of this light first from a preacher who traveled the countryside on horseback, one of Mr. Whitefield's followers, who spoke with great warmth and passion of the holy spirit dwelling in all God's creatures. True religion, he proclaimed in that exhorting style of Methodists and Baptists, began with the heart's love for God. With a mind cleansed of sinfulness and a heart converted to cultivating the spark of divinity within, any man, high or low, may enter the sacred Kingdom. From the day I listened, enraptured by the preacher's words, by truths he revealed both gloriously new and achingly familiar, I strove to make myself worthy of salvation. Salvation bought by the precious blood Jesus shed for us all. So touched was I by the affecting message, I apprenticed myself to the preacher and soon afterward took to the road to spread the Lord's good news.

I chose a modest vineyard to suit my modest powers. I believed God had a plan for me, a simple plan to which I needed only to conform in order to obtain my best chance of happiness in this world and the next. I harbored no ambition to convert great multitudes, nor to occupy the pulpit of a grand church. Any man who aims too high imperils his soul, and for a man of color such overreaching is doubly dangerous. Life and limb in jeopardy as well as his immortal part.

Young, unmarried, of a hearty constitution — except for these feet, the everlasting, bunioned cross of these large Negro feet — I could travel in the backcountry among the isolated, far-flung farms and holdings. Live off the bounty of the land and occasional charity from those I served. During the seasons of planting or harvesting I might reside some weeks at a time in a small community, earning my keep by toiling in the fields, assembling a tiny following as news circulated of my preaching, whose style, if I may say without boasting, pleased many. To supply the needs I couldn't expect my bare-bones folk to provide — clothes, tools, a Bible, candles, spectacles for my nearsighted eyes, boots for my long-suffering African feet — I would chop wood, drive a wagon, skills I had learned tolerably well when my former master hired me out to his neighbors.

Though my precious family was gone, though I sorely miss them to this day, I believed God in his infinite mercy had granted me entrance into another circle of kindred spirits, those who had found His light within themselves and struggled to be worthy of His grace.

To an unwise degree, perhaps, I was content with the small rigors and triumphs of my life, believed I occupied a niche that Providence had intended for me. I settled outside Philadelphia, near a little rural village, a peaceful, sleepy, unhurried place where I could find employment and ample opportunity for my real vocation of converting souls. But while we slept, the city descended upon us. A drifting city of sin, of makeshift shelters and homeless souls and fear and hate.

I learned in rapid, whispered exchanges with coach drivers and footmen the plight of the city's Africans.

We are being blamed in the newspapers. They say we are immune to the fever and require no assistance. They say black slaves, refugees from the troubles in Haiti, brought the fever to these shores. Mark my word, it is the contagion of freedom they fear. The lie of our immunity, the blame foisted upon us, are preposterous, cowardly excuses for beating us, denying us employment, avoiding our stalls and goods, revoking our hard-won rights. We are slaves again, impressed in crews that must nurse the sick, bury the dead.

The whites of our village were ignorant of these outrages, as they were, if I may say so, of most matters beyond tending their fields and livestock. Somehow the black people of my acquaintance, equally absorbed and oppressed by the never-ending labor of eking out a precarious living, were not unfamiliar with the hardships besetting their urban brethren. I've often wondered how such news travels, and so accurately and swiftly. Perhaps through our African blood. Its ancient excitability refined by tribal drums. An acuteness of ear no other race can match. More likely in this instance my African brethren learned what they needed to know from the hostile stares of white newcomers to our neighborhood. Knowledge was communicated amongst us just as unspoken attitudes were passed from one white person to another in daily intercourse.

Though cruel traditions, the worst being exclusion from all but one row of benches in St. Matthew's, reminded us daily that whites deemed us an inferior race, we had managed to live side by side with them, relatively free of turmoil, as long as certain lines weren't trespassed. All of us, black and white, equally marooned by poverty, by the stark necessities of our lives. No spare time for the frivolity of race hate. Then the fear, anger, arrogance and cold distance of city-dwellers fleeing the plague soured our simple truce.

As a youth I'd lived as a slave, suffered that status under one cruel, one generous master, endured slavery daily. Like plague, *slave* much more than a word to me. More. Worse. I understood slavery's evil, yet it seemed no more terrible than this new condition white people were contriving for the so-called free blacks in the city. If rumors held any truth, we had been declared guilty, sentenced to die for the crime of plague. Though we too were its victims. Though we fought valiantly, desperately, to save ourselves and others from its ravages. Fought to rescue a city that with one hand commandeered our services while the other waved us away, condemning us to exile and ruin.

Loath as I was to desert my scattered flock, I also felt compelled to go to the assistance of my brethren in the city. I struggled with the choice. Resisted within myself a bitter, growing awareness of skin color, a choking rage at men who employed it to sunder God's kingdom. On my knees I sought guidance. Argued with myself and prayed, but suspicion and resentment of a white face, simply because it was white, festered like a canker sore beneath my skin. Dire events conspired to remove my choices. And it was no boon when, finally, I had no choice.

After a long, harsh winter, spring had burst upon us in an unceasing round of storms. We woke to rain. Rain battered us to sleep, soaked our dreams. Low-lying areas were flooded. Fields became marshes. A season of late planting, clouds of insects fiercer and more voracious than usual, as if hatched knowing their season of feeding and breeding had been foreshortened by winter's prolonged grip on the land. Then July heat sudden and intense. An anvil our bodies were laid upon and pounded. To increase our woes, a seemingly endless drought after the flood. Muddy roads turned to dusty ditches, cracked and furrowed. August a month of white skies. Breezeless calm. Heavy air. Lakes shrinking from their banks. Ponds drying up altogether. A flat glaze stilling the rivers and streams, the water's skin glared, seamless, hard as ice.

On one of those stifling August afternoons after the city had begun to invade the peaceful precincts of our neighborhood, as I trekked toward a remote valley where two farms nestled, their families unconverted to the truth of the inner light, I noticed a dark speck far ahead of me shimmering on the horizon. Perhaps a trick of the sun. Perhaps a person. Perhaps a mote of dust in my eye, or a drop of sweat glued to my lashes. A womanshape as I drew closer. Pedestal of flowing skirts. Slim-backed and slim-waisted, carriage erect as if she's balancing a load atop the turban wrapped around her head. Beneath the pinch of waist, a refugee's resigned gait, the numb plod over endless leagues that brings you no closer to a destination, leagues that are your destination, step after heavy step on a road going nowhere, sapping your strength, exhausting your will to go further.

She appears and disappears when the road bends, rises or falls. Larger, more distinct on a straight, flat stretch, as my purposeful strides outstrip her faltering ones. Before I see the telltale bundle straddling her hip, the baby secured there in the African manner, I know she is an African woman. Her walk leaves no doubt. A supple flow that exhaustion cannot extinguish. Even if she falls, she'll fall gracefully.

She pauses. Sways. Has weariness consumed the last of her strength. Will she collapse onto the parched grass bordering the hard-packed earth of this track. No. She pushes on. Her shoulders echo the subtle swing of her hips, her body possessing itself again.

I did not see her dance, and the market basket on her head was invisible, but these African parts of her were as real as the raw, naked feet protruding from her gown when finally, near the crest of a punishing grade, I overtook her.

She sat with her back against a tree, legs extended straight before her. Long, narrow feet they were, grime-crusted, bleeding. Dusty soles dark as her sable ankles. Not the iron-callused feet of a country woman. A lady's feet, or more likely the feet of a lady's maid, given the woman's color, the neat cut of her garments, fashioned from sturdy linen, plain in style, uncolorful so no guest's eye might be enticed to stray from the finery of her mistress.

A delicate foot, poorly served by rough, rural paths. An indoor foot, a foot for silk slippers or soft leather boots with raised heels and many buttons. A foot weeping now. Soot-streaked, bloody tears, and I wished for a basin of cool water in my sack. I wanted to kneel beside her, bathe away the misery, listen to her recite the tale of her misfortune, learn what trials had brought her hence, her good clothes filthy and in tatters, city stockings and city shoes shredded clean away from her bare feet.

I could say more about her battered feet. They told a story of their own. When I recall the sweltering day, the dusty road, our meeting, the strange events that ensued, I know there will be a point when the image of those tender, bruised feet materializes. They implore me to deal with them, stir me as they did that day. Then I must choose to go on with my story or digress. Endlessly digress, because if I follow where her feet lead, I will enter her skin and then there is no end, only the maze of her in which I lose myself forever.

So I will not call the feet *hers*. Just feet. When I saw where the woman had dropped, the vast black network of branches overhead, the apron of roots erupting through the soil, the feet, in truth, did not seem to belong to her. She seemed anciently planted in the earth. The bare feet a separate growth, fresh shoots from the giant tree, dark tentacles that had plunged underground until they cleared the woman's gown. Feet as new on the earth as a child's. Familiar as my own feet or hands, yet who could guess what fate intends for them. I could reach out and touch her, but I'd never know her touch. Never know how the ground feels to her heels and toes, how the world makes her feel.

She has undone the bundle from her hip. It rests between her legs in the hollow of the gown, as she rests in the lap of roots. The oak throws a canopy of shade. Stepping under it is like entering a cellar. Until I'm standing a few feet from her I don't see the infant's pale face, the chaos of golden curls.

The feet, I'm sure now, not hers. Wooden feet carved and painted by some cunning craftsman to beguile her into believing she still owns actual feet at the ends of her limbs, flesh-and-blood feet with the power to move her from place to place.

For a moment it seemed the entire figure might be some kind of life-size doll propped against the tree. So little did she stir. Not a sound or nod or blink. Arms limp on either side of her body. Carved child quiet in her lap. Chin tucked against a bosom neither rising nor falling with the rhythm of breath.

Though the vital force appeared unnaturally suspended, I never feared she was dead. Enchanted by a wizard's spell, perhaps, but not dead. The scent of her too fierce. Her skin too hot and wet.

Since you know the story at least as well as I know it, I'm tempted to skip ahead. But then I lose something of you. We separate. I don't get to hear the questions you might ask: how did we find the lake. Which one of us knew its location. How long did we walk to arrive on its shore. When I omit parts of the story, do I relinquish my hold on you. When the tale jumps to a different place, where do you go. Promise you will tell me someday. I pray you are not disappointed when I leave things out. Promise we can return together and sort out what's missing. I can't bear to think this single telling is my last chance, my only chance to be here with you.

How long have I been sitting on this bed watching you. How many times have I begun this story. Reaching out again and again.

Are you offering me your foot to touch. Or are you sleeping. Your bare foot straying from the covers, in another story perhaps, far from here, a stranger's dream I can't enter even if I dared to stroke your foot, take it in both my hands and lift it to my lips.

The question remains. When I stumble, will you assist me, abide with me. Will you share the story with me, dream it all again in your own words. The parts I say, the parts I don't or can't.

On that August day, thunder portended no rain. Hunger rumbling in my stomach huge as the ocean. White sky swollen to the bursting point, a mother's breast, no lips to suck it.

She unwound rags from the child's body, exposing the soiled remnant of a blue silk chemise, disintegrating in her hands as she drew it up and over the baby's arms, the cap of gold curls. A stick child. She turned it face down, hiding the grotesquely distended belly. Licking her little finger, she used it to groom the crack of the baby's backside, withered as an ancient man's.

Lookee how dirty, sir. Must bath dis poor child. She patted. Cooed. Combed her fingers through yellow hair dry as a doll's.

Him tired. Mama's baby tired, tired, tired. Poor hair nappy bad. Poor pretty hair.

She slowly massaged the unmoving body. Surely a corpse, he thought, its stillness and pallor accentuated by the contrast of her dark fingers rubbing, squeezing, stroking. Dead how long. And did this woman know it. Had grief banished reason.

Could she be the child's mother. He'd seen whiter babies with darker mothers.

Must washee. Puttee cradle for sleep.

Be kind dis poor woman, sir. Help dis woman. Mistress gib penny you come back door say helpee dis poor woman.

Yes, madam. I'm sorry. So sorry. God bless you, madam. May God have mercy on this child's blameless soul. Depend on me, madam. I will do all in my power to assist you.

Oh, tankee, sir. Yes. Yes. Pretty white word in black mouth. Takee baby, sir. This woman get sore behind off ground.

He remembers the cabin, the ax. Shouting *no no no* to himself even as he reached for the cobwebbed handle. Now he is reaching for the child and the voice warns him again. Something was going to happen and he didn't understand exactly what it was, had no words to describe it, but it didn't matter, the noes didn't matter, then or now, because he'd already crossed a threshold, and there was no turning back.

Her feet moving again, a whisper behind him in the withered grass. For a while he followed hints of a path. It meandered east, away from the main road, the giant, solitary oak, crossed a clearing, then cut through scraggly brush and new growth that hid groundcover blackened by fire. At the end of an abandoned pasture the path vanishes, dividing into a delta of game trails skittering deeper into the forest. The man and woman pick their way along the rocky bed of a dry creek at the base of a hill, then ascend a steep shoulder that after a quarter mile narrows abruptly and sends them skidding through shale, dropping them into the vast droning of locusts, a cool darkness among black stems of evergreens whose layered branches both obscure the sky and admit dappled shafts of light.

He knew the backways and byways of the wilderness. More than once he'd staked his life on unfrequented shortcuts that would bring him to the warmth of a fireplace, the shelter of a barn before a snowstorm trapped him in open country. Though he'd never fired a musket, he fished, set traps and snares, considered himself adept at foraging from the land what he needed to survive. The map he carried in his head guided him accurately, efficiently, through a landscape of gently rolling fields and meadows couched in almost impenetrable tracts of virgin forest. Thickets of foothills, and beyond them, rippling one after another, rows of blue mountains, flat on the horizon, as if cut from paper. He knew the animals, had acquainted himself with their habits and habitats. Knew patches of wild berries, navigable streams, boiling rapids in steep gorges that would rip a canoe apart. Where and how far a team and wagon could be trusted. The location of cliff-high waterfalls with rainbows snared in webs of spray and spume. Crystal lakes hidden in the hills, so deep and still even his silent prayers profaned them.

As well as he knew the land, each time he ventured an ell from his customary routes, he became a stranger. The unknown gobbled up the known, spit it out quicker than he could holler his name. The known as useless as a stone hurled at a blizzard bearing down on his heels.

No semblance of a trail now. Each step plunges them deeper into country he'd never walked. The unknown swallowed you, set you adrift. Lost, he admitted. Lost as the soul of this dead child till God calls it home.

Was he leading the woman or was she driving him, behind him but in control, her bare feet punching like fists into dense undergrowth. The child tucked in the crook of his arm. A second heart. An icy lump of heart. Chilly sweat soaking his shirt where the small body pressed. Afraid of dropping it, afraid of squeezing too tight. The child burning a hole through him. A tunnel for his eyes to stare back and meet hers boring forward. Blind woman. Blind man. Like lovers in a dark bed, tracking each other by the noises they make. The unknown a wind rushing through the cavity in his chest. He doesn't know where he's going. He's sure, sure of that. Sure they'll wind up exactly where they must.

How did you find the water. How did you know.

Do you know. Do you ever know know know.

It could have been the beginning of time. Dropped in a glade in the primeval forest.

How long did they walk. The woman, the man with a dead child pressed under the arm he hugs to himself like a broken wing. He didn't want to drop her child, feared crushing it, wound up cupping its cold bottom so the baby rode straddling his hand as it had straddled the woman's hip. He cannot remember how long. Why should that detail matter now. Minutes. Days. No time he can reckon with clock or calendar. He'd asked his mother how much salt in the stew she was preparing for the master's supper and she'd laughed. The right much. That's how much. Now go on away from here pestering me, boy.

He remembers many places, many people crowded into a dreamlike whirl as he led her through the woods. A lifetime's worth of rooms, cities, black pools beside the sea, a cavern under the mountains, places they looped in and out of on their journey toward the water. It took as long as a trek across a continent in a caravan of ox-drawn wagons, it was as brief as stepping through an open door.

The only thing he's sure of now is that they found the water. A lake a mile or so across, its length hidden by the tree-lined shoulders of a cove they'd emerged from the woods to find opening before them. The tide of drought had pulled the water away from its banks, exposing a ledge of boulders and overhanging trees, then more rocks, smaller, speckled, then a seam of smooth-pebbled gravel bordering the sand. Sand that in an ordinary season would be submerged, now a golden strip of beach.

He understood, without knowing why, that this was as far as they needed to go. This quiet crescent of lake he was viewing for the first time. Perhaps no human eyes have seen it before. He is lost. No familiar landmarks. The opposite shore, like this one, lined with trees, their upside-down, black-green reflections in the water. The sun's height, its position in the sky, the disposition of shadows around him and on the far bank, told him something about the moment, about time of day, the cardinal directions, nothing about how or why he'd arrived here. Nor how much of his life the journey had consumed.

A breeze rising off the water is a blessing. One, two whispers, then it's gone. He's drenched with sweat. His chest heaves. Has he been running. Running away from the burden clutched in his arm. How could an exhausted, footsore woman keep up if he'd been running. Why would he drive himself like a fool in this heat, over the unsteadfast footing of the forest floor. Yet he recalls the sound of heavy footfalls, panting, piles of leaves exploding, cracking branches. They were escaping together, a family on the run. Men on horseback with baying hounds pursued them. They must plunge deeper into the forest, slip into briars and tangled undergrowth where horses can't follow, splash through marsh and swamp so the slobber-jowled dogs will lose their scent.

From where he stands he can peer down into the lake. The water is clear and still. After the border of pebbles, the sandy bottom slopes gently. It holds the frozen impression of ripples that on other days, in other times, have plied the surface. Sunlight stripes the water, repeating the pattern of ridges petrified below in the sand.

Birds cheep, trill, whistle, shriek. The wall of boulders rimming the bank is breached occasionally where black, marshy pools have scooped out pockets of land. There, instead of drooping branches and bristling undergrowth, cattail reeds cluster at the water's edge, tall and precise. A buzz and drone of insects closer at hand, more intimate than the cries of birds. Dragonflies longer than his finger are shining darts, blue and green, a glittering whir of translucent doubled wings.

Now, she says.

He didn't want to surrender the child. Was she its mother. What did she intend. What would his God have him do. Pray for the baby's soul. Bury its mortal remains. Perhaps if they laid it down in this bright water, it would paddle off. Miraculously revived, like God's son.

He releases the baby into her arms. A boy. A girl. Its tiny sex mashed against his hand as he'd carried it through the woods, but he couldn't tell. Both. Neither. What matter now.

The woman as agile as she is graceful clambered over the rocks, across the necklace of polished stones. Her bare toes sink into damp sand. Kneeling, she lays the child on the sling that had become a blanket after she'd unwound it from her hips.

He moves closer. Down the slight incline, shuffing his feet through roots, weeds, black, black dirt that would be mud most summers. Closer to the source of the precious whisper of fresh air. He mounts a rock the shape, color and texture of a turtle shell. Closer to her.

Her back is toward him. The slim back he remembers materializing on the road, above the flared column of gown and petticoat. Her arms bare now. The shawl that had draped her shoulders in spite of the heat lies on the sand, next to the baby on its blanket. Bony arms, lean-muscled, the image of wiry strength. Arms trim and elegant as her feet. She unfastens the turban. So much cloth in all this heat. Wound round her head, in gown, petticoat, shift, apron, shawl, the blanket she'd fashioned into a sling around her hips. An extravagance of cotton, linen, wool, a madness of material in these impossibly hot days. Like him she was a refugee. Dressed with a refugee's grimness for all seasons. Bundled into the pack on his back were rags he'd wrap round himself after the first frosts. In the icy wind and rain and snow these layers covering her, like his, would be woefully inadequate. Inappropriate then as now.

She tilts her head, shrugs, and the head kerchief lands at her feet. Her skull is naked, innocent of hair as the soles of her feet. He's shocked at first. He's never seen a bald woman. Even the old grannies and aunties retained some ghost of hair when he surprised them without their headwraps. Fuzzy down, clumps, tetters, curls, wisps, a frizzy snow-white cloud. As soon as he realized what he was seeing, the newness of it, the starkness, he couldn't imagine the woman's head any other way. No texture, length or color of hair could enhance her bare skull. Gleaming sweat heightens the drama of bone.

Slowly she undresses. Stares into the water after her whole body's naked as her head. Has she forgotten he's behind her. Does she care. Why should she. Why does her nakedness, her sex, matter any more or less than the child's.

As if she's decided to answer all his questions at once, she moves a few yards from her discarded clothes, squats and pisses, glancing once over her shoulder toward the rock on which he stands. He couldn't look away fast enough to miss her eyes on him, nor pretend his aren't on her, nor miss the instant glance away, her eyes returning to the dreamy business of a long, long pee in the sand.

Her feet print a second trail, paralleling then joining the first. She drops to one knee again. Gathers the child in her arms. Mutters indistinguishable sounds to it as she strides into the water. Slowly, deeper and deeper, stirring ripples behind and before her as one leg then the other pushes through the water. Water rises to her thighs, her waist, covers her breasts, the baby in her arms, water finally closing over the dark glisten of her skull.

I was frozen where I stood. How long I remained there, I can't say. At least till night, I believe, because I remember stars. The black vault of heaven's arch over the trees, the water. A sky full of stars. Not the crisp pinpoints of a winter's night. Summer heat had softened their edges. Squashed stars, bleeding stars, the texture of dandelion crowns gone to seed, just before the wind disperses them.

I stood at least through a night, perhaps many more. No name for the time. I can't supply a measure for it any more than I can say how long we trekked to reach the lake. The most accurate accounting of how long I spent gazing after her, silent, not believing I'd stood there and watched her sink, watched the water close over her head, the circles one within the other, expanding from the final dark trace of her — all I can say to clarify how much time passed is this: it happened and I was there and now I'm here telling you.

She strolled to the middle of the lake — disappeared — and you watched.

No. Not the middle. More like twenty, thirty paces. Far from the middle.

Middle. Smiddle. Diddle-dum. The point is, you watched. Did you try to save her? No. You watched.

More waiting than watching. I expected her to pop up from the water any moment.

Any moment. Any moment, you say. Any moment after she'd been gone five minutes, an hour, all night.

Yes. I didn't wait long enough. I lost faith. Deserted her. She trusted me, asked me to help, but I didn't wait long enough.

You weren't waiting for her. What you call waiting for her was really letting her go. Watching her drown. A poor, distracted soul who'd lost her baby and you allowed her to destroy herself.

No. No. She was washing the child. She asked me to find water so she could bathe it, prepare the child for its long journey. She accompanied it part of the way. Like a prayer. She loved the child and couldn't let go until she was certain it was safely on its way home.

You. You are the child. Spinning fanciful tales.

She returned. I know she did. If I'd waited, I might have found you sooner. Before it was too late.

Perhaps it's not too late. Perhaps it never is.

The hour is late now. One of them will be tapping on the ladder. You'll leave and I'll be stranded here wondering about the plague. Your decision to go or not go to the city. You began by saying you were torn twixt town and country, black and white. An anger rising in you toward the whites. Symptoms of the fever poisoning your village. You see how well I listen. You must take pains to reward my diligence.

Then a woman and child enter your story. They drown, or, as you'll have it, they disappear in a lake. You watch. Beg pardon, you wait. Either way, I am no closer to Philadelphia. You stop your story. Sigh like one who's lost a true love. Like some lady's fragile, bejeweled music box finished chiming its sentimental ditty. Useless till the lady winds it up again with the tiny gold key on a gold thread round her delicate neck. Her swannish neck. Swoonish neck.

Come. You owe me, sir, a trip to Philadelphia. Love's another story.

Philadelphia. Love is buried in its name, you know.

Love. Love, sir. Surely not during the season of plague. A most unlovely time, by your word.

Very little love. Yes. Yes. But love was there. The city would not have survived without it.

The woman I overtook on the road leads us back to Philadelphia. She was the only person in her master's house who loved the child enough to accompany it into the deadly city streets and beyond, after it had been infected with the fever.

Her master had barricaded himself, his wife, his sons and their families behind the walls of his grand mansion to wait out the siege of plague. He'd set his house apart, as if wealth and pride and ruthlessness were proof against the fever. A prominent physician had exiled himself with the rich man's family. He was a quarantiner, one of the medical fraternity who believed the fatal sickness spread through contact with the afflicted. Thus no one was allowed to enter or leave the mansion, not even merchants who delivered provisions. When the child displayed the unmistakable first signs of fever, on the physician's advice they cast it out like a leper from amongst them.

I heard this story from many lips in Philadelphia. It had become a popular parable of sorts. The grand house cast as a castle of arrogance, callousness and greed. Threats shouted down from barred windows at any who dared approach. A troop of liveried servants who rushed out one day and beat with sticks a crowd of beggars who'd broken into the courtyard, only to discover, after they'd thrashed the hapless intruders, that they too were locked out. Not a crumb spared for a starving widow, infant at her shriveled breast, who'd crawled into the stable. Rumor has it the inhabitants of the mansion engaged in frenzied feasting and unnatural pleasures, indulging their carnal appetites unashamedly while corpses piled up around the granite walls. As you might guess, to round the tale, God's judgment swiftly descended upon the barred mansion. After the lastborn had been so crudely expelled, one by one in rapid succession, from youngest to oldest, everyone hiding in the mansion was stricken with fever.

Cries for help rained from the windows. Voices weakened by fever pleading, whining. A fortune offered to anyone who would enter the stout gates and tend the sick, remove the dead. A great stench issued from its marble chambers, overpowering even the foul miasma the city's air had become in the season of plague. The grand house an abode of the dead and dying no one would go near.

Another twist to the tale, a female servant, a slave, who so loved the newest child in the family she chose to leave the fortressed dwelling and care for the sick infant after her masters had decided unanimously to abandon it beyond the walls.

They say the young African woman who had always been a shy and dutiful sort of mouse suddenly quit her previous character, rose up on her hind legs and forbade her masters to carry out their plan. No. No, she admonished. Dare not destroy your own off-spring. Your future. Your hope. You must risk all to save this help-less, innocent babe. Once I heard the tale recited as if the teller herself had been a family retainer, privy to a scene in the opu-lent dining room as the humble slave girl confronted her betters. Enough wine already consumed to make them wonder if this saucy black wench chastising them was real or some devil-sent apparition.

You must not, you cannot commit this terrible deed, she ex-horts. And then the slave, not much older than a child herself, threatens her masters with prophecy.

I beseech you. Spare yourselves the wrath of God. He is watch-ing. His eye penetrates even here in this stony citadel of plenty and power. God's wrath shall fall full upon you if you abandon your own flesh and blood.

A commendable performance by the slave girl and also by the maid who imitated for an audience of us colored folk the slave's speech to her masters. Much flourishing of hands, Cassandra-like flashing of eyes, noble sentiments declaimed. I'd heard, however, from other sources, that the African girl who ran off with the sick child was *bozal*, fresh from the West Indies. Her speech a barely intelligible Negro English quite inadequate for the high-flown sentiments and ringing imprecations delivered by the lady's maid imagining herself in the other's shoes. I think the servant woman who performed the tale was saying to her fellow sufferers what she'd always yearned to say to her masters. Employing, at last, the language she'd so arduously learned and adopted, to express in this rare instance what was truly in her heart.

When I pieced together many versions of the tale, the slave girl's broken, *bozal* English, the child's fatal illness, its lustrous crown of golden curls, the slave's ebony hue, her youth and come-liness, her African habits, it became clear to me they could be the pair I'd met on the road.

You can imagine my astonishment. Each time I heard about a child put out to die, a loving servant who risked her life for its sake, I remembered them, my two ill-fated companions. I was tempted to add the story's last chapter. The strange twist. The sad conclusion.

However, I couldn't tell the rest without disclosing my role. Without implicating myself. Or at the very least explaining myself. And I was not prepared to try.

Besides, learning their history had changed my understanding of woman and child. Where should my story start, where end. I couldn't complete tales I heard from others, because clearly the story wasn't over. Nothing had ended. Mystery had deepened. What I thought I knew once, had changed. The woman and baby had disappeared. Yes. The water had closed over her head. Yes. But only like a curtain between acts. There I was in Philadelphia, the waters parting, her figure rising again.

Though I'd deserted her, I was still waiting. Eventually, I'd stepped down off the rock at the edge of the lake, traveled to the city, but I never stopped expecting to see her. Aching, I admit now, aching for another glimpse. Another chance. A glimpse of her hand or foot, her scent preserved on a piece of clothing. I wondered what I might discover if I ransacked the evil mansion she'd fled. Perhaps something of hers hidden away, a bundle or bag she couldn't take the night she stole the child. In the squalid wreckage of her master's house, what was hers would be preserved pure, incorruptible, like a saint's body in its coffin. If I sifted through its rotting chambers, what would I find in the phantom castle.

In Philadelphia numerous versions of the tale competed. The African girl was the baby's mother, its father her master's roguish ne'er-do-well youngest son. Baby thus the master's bastard grandchild. Some said the son's wife not fruitful herself and was shamed and bullied into accepting the slave's pale child as her own offspring. Or the child a by-blow of the goatish patriarch himself, one more living monument to his vigor and vitality, a daughter in this version, sired upon a female slave, herself his daughter. Or the child of an enslaved African servant and a man who'd purchased his freedom. Brown husband and wife, their baby inexplicably fair-skinned, golden-haired, a sign from birth of its unnatural fate. In another tale the woman's unconquerable love for husband and son confirmed by countless acts of selfless dedication and courage. With her husband first forced to fight Frenchmen and Indians in Canada, then enlisting during the Rebellion to fight the British, then incarcerated on a prisoner-of-war ship in New York harbor, finally returning home, but in a few years ordered away again, this time commandeered to battle the ravages of plague as nurse and driver of the dead carts — she raises their son alone. Refuses to surrender him to the fatal fever, steals away with him at night, seeking her husband, determined to unite the family at last.

I believed each story. My way of reckoning learned from the old African people, who said all stories are true. What mattered was that I had found her again. After the killing night, the night whites attacked the black people of my village, I thought God sent me to Philadelphia to tame my murderous rage, my longing for revenge. Instead of abandoning me, letting the anger in my heart destroy me, finishing the work of enemies who'd missed me during the night of slaughter, God, I believed, had preserved me to aid my brethren, to perform my Christian duty to those in dire need.

I prayed I would learn in Philadelphia to quell the bitterness in my heart. I would confront again the worst of the whites and teach myself that their worst was no better or worse than mine, the sinful nature all God's children must strive to overcome. I would not repay evil with evil. I would humbly aid all who would accept my assistance. Thus I understood my mission to the city. Believed my mind's blind eye had made me privy to God's plan for me. So I thought. Until she reappeared. And then I knew my heart had led me all along. Not duty but love had drawn me to Philadelphia. To you.

There's the tap-tap-tapping. You don't hear it, do you. You're asleep, aren't you. One last word tonight. I'll whisper it into your dreaming. May it take root there. One soft, soft whispered word. So no one at the bottom of the ladder overhears. So you, dear one, if you're teasing and only pretending sleep, won't hear.

Sometimes when we meet to thrash out this business, going backward in the story is more important than proceeding forward.

Do we have a choice, my friend. I thought stories always go backward.

Backward to go forward. Forward to go back. Yes. Please be patient with me. I need to tell you about an incident that occurred before she disappeared into the lake. Before I followed her to Philadelphia. Before plague had driven city people to seek refuge in the peaceful environs of the countryside where I wandered preaching the word of God.

Only after I'd lost her did I realize I'd met her before. A year or so after a storm had spit me near the village of Radnor. She was someone I'd seen previously, briefly, before the blistering summer day on the road when I caught up with her and the doomed child. I simply hadn't connected the two occasions. Why I didn't recognize her immediately I cannot say. No child with her the first time I saw her and our first meeting was brief, brief, not even long enough for me to form a distinct impression of her face. Yet after I'd lost her the second time, I grew certain the woman on the road and the woman I must tell you about now were the same person. I began to recall more and more about her as I rehearsed the circumstances of our first meeting. No doubt about it. She had returned. And because she'd returned once, she could return again, even from the waters where she'd carried her child. If she'd returned once, she could again, and would, as real in this floating world where I sit talking to you as she is in my iron memories.

Bear with me. Let me relate to you our first meeting, itself also, strangely, a return. To memory, possibility, life. As all stories are.

She returns on the Lord's day. Or rather the day once a week honored as the Lord's. At a time when I still fervently believed all days were His, believed our every breath, our every moment on this earth depended on God's grace, His mercy, His compassion for benighted, stiff-necked creatures such as we are, unworthy of His blessings, undeserving of the precious blood of Jesus, our Savior, His only begotten son. An October Sunday in the year of our Lord 1792.

Like the whale delivering Jonah, a snowstorm had deposited me more dead than alive near the village of Radnor, a market town in a sparsely populated region hemmed in by mountainous terrain and forests, twelve miles from Philadelphia.

Mr. Stubbs and his wife had rescued me from the storm, taken me into their household. I owed my life to them, and readily accepted Mr. Stubbs' offer of employment. An added incentive was the opportunity I was afforded to gather round me a settled congregation. I thought I might stay a few months, but resided there nearly two years. Of this African Stubbs, who wasn't really Stubbs, and his Englishwoman, who posed as the wife of the actual Stubbs, their unusual history, peregrinations, and sudden, tragic end, more later. It suffices now to say I suffered a period of unexpected twists and turnings, an improbable, soul-wrenching time, and the Sunday I wish to describe no exception to the precipitous ups and downs of fortune marking my stay in Radnor.

The Sunday I'm recalling began badly. Flashing lights beset me the instant I awakened in Stubbs' barn. Lights swarmed like insects round my head, the storm before the calm before the storm, so to speak. Let me explain. I suffer strange falling fits. A pattern announces them.

First, a storm of frenzied, darting and streaking lights. Soundless fireworks I might enjoy if I didn't dread the awful calm, the second storm of falling fit, those lights presage.

Flashing lights, then a stifling calm. My skull empties, hollow as a drum. An emptiness pushes against the bones of my face as a bursting fullness would. My teeth ache. Imagine your skin throbbing at the highest pitch of receptivity, a thrilling alertness exhausting you. Now conceive a dullness of the senses just as exhausting. A deadly, mired, Sargasso Sea calm rendering you dry-mouthed, immobile. A yawning emptiness stretching from the center of your being outward to the ends of the earth. An eternity of waiting compressed into this becalmed state of bloated stillness. Your mind prays for an explosion that never comes, won't come till in its own good time it snatches you by the seat of your breeches and hurls you senseless to the ground.

I faint dead away. Awaken to the second storm. Then I'm a pretty sight, indeed. Wall-eyed. Slobbering. Gagging. Fingers digging my tongue out of my mouth so I don't chew it or swallow it. Barking like a dog. A cat meowing. These noises and worse — demon hisses, witch howls, the coarsest tavern oaths, they tell me, issuing in a vicious stream from my lips. A bedlamite writhing on the ground. Spitting. Fouling myself. Limbs twitching uncontrollably. A worm from hell. An insect some kind soul should stomp upon and put out of its misery.

Lights, calm, senselessness and then a boulder is rolled aside and I'm exposed. A pitiful, curling grub.

I have such an undressing to anticipate when a storm of lights no one else can see batters me. When the lights birth an unnatural calm. When darkness engulfs me and rioting devils possess my soul.

Fear of a fit affects me almost as much as the event itself. Though irresistible, the fits shame me, unman me. Rolling about in the dirt till I gather a crowd of curious onlookers. I can hear their gasps and screams, their raillery and merriment now.

The fainting fits are infrequent and short-lived. When they end, after the trembling ceases, after I regain my balance and begin to compose myself, I'm vouchsafed a startling clarity of vision. In a breath I go from hell on earth to paradise. Great relaxation floods my being. Gentle fingers unknot me. Strand by strangled strand. I'm freed to contemplate the mysteries of creation.

Every leaf shines forth. Splendor shimmering in every detail of creation. I glimpse a world sweet as it must have been, and still is, if we had but eyes to see it, before the Fall.

Words can't describe the clarity. Suffice to say I *see*. For a brief, blessed interval a glorious seeing restores the world to me. Restores me to the world.

On the October Sunday in question, after whirling lights had greeted me, neither calm nor a second storm ensued. I sipped cool water from the gourd beside my straw pallet. As is often the case, the cycle had been broken. Forces I could not control nor understand had prevented a full-blown attack. As was my habit then, I thanked God for sparing me pain and humiliation. Though a part of me always regretted the missed opportunity of clear-seeing, I was grateful that morning not to pay the awful, soul-shriveling price the fits exact.

A fit avoided. Or so it seemed. Though I have fainted dead away three times in one week, months may separate spells. The fits as vexingly unpredictable as they are overpowering. Spinning lights a fickle signal. The flashes may subside with no consequence or they may return in earnest hours later, bringing or not bringing the suffocating calm, a fit in their wake. Rather than sighing with relief when the lights die, I'm dogged by foreboding. Become anxious, wary. Each visitation of flashes a reminder of my helplessness. False alarms can poison whole days.

I'm telling you my secrets — how I lost her, how I stole from a dying man, how devils possess me. What in turn have you revealed. Will this abundant divulging of my secrets embarrass you into sharing yours. Tit for tat. Or will my disclosures frighten you away.

The day she returned began with a warning. If a fit was coming on, I preferred not to be abroad in public, but I was determined that morning to attend, as had become my custom, St. Matthew's, the village church.

St. Matthew's, the village's largest structure, serves also as a meetinghouse, school, and during the Indian wars, as gunports round the walls testify, doubled as a fortress. The church is pastored by the Reverend Doctor Amos Parker, a new arrival from England. A fair-haired, thin, tall, sallow man, stiff in comportment and utterance. One of Britain's disgruntled exports to our shores, who will scowl and find fault until that island's gray temperament rules our green wilderness. One who would replace our weather with theirs.

He is not, I assure you, what attracted me to St. Matthew's. His dry sermons barely distinguishable one from the other. He scolds rather than rejoices. Though his uninspired lectures touch no heart with their *submit, submit, duty, duty* whine, the Holy Spirit, in spite of the dour cleric's mumbling, would now and then descend upon a parishioner. Woe unto the pilgrim who dares celebrate the Lord's presence. An abomination. Blasphemy, cries the minister. No joy permitted here. No showing forth of the inner light. Who dares bypass God's bespectacled gatekeeper. Who offends the dignity of the church by feasting at the Lord's bounteous table instead of pecking and scratching among the dry grains of *thou shalt not* Doctor Parker scatters like a chicken farmer for his flock.

Parker makes it a special point to guard against fanatical expressions or wild, enthusiastic displays. One Sunday he related the heroic tale of a summary process he took with a certain black matron, who with many extravagant gestures in her *love-feast*, as he called it, cried out that she was Young King Jesus. He bade her take her seat and read her out of membership, stating that in his congregation he would not abide such wild fanatics.

With a warmth unusual for him, Parker censured from the pulpit what many others have welcomed as a much-needed religious awakening. He railed against itinerant preachers such as myself who take to the highways and byways to feed the common people's hunger for spiritual nourishment and religious instruction. The efforts of Baptists and Methodists — *latitudinarians*, in his learned, pursed-lip lingo — to open the doors of the church to all who would enter weakens the church, he said. Vagabond preachers, he declared, cast an undiscriminating net, drawing unsavory types to the bosom of the church, including Negroes free and slave, women, the shiftless and untutored, whose undisciplined enthusiasm mocked true faith. When emotion not reason rules, he claimed, louts catechized today dare debate scripture with bishops tomorrow.

I didn't need to go to St. Matthew's to find God on Sunday and wondered each time I sat in that drafty barn why some people would try His patience with such hypocritical airs of saintliness — angels inside St. Matthew's, devils the instant they exit. My sole reason for attending services there was the opportunity afforded for fellowship with my African brethren.

Only a handful of blacks worshiped at St. Matthew's. Not enough to fill the last two rows at the back of the church, designated for us. Plenty of room for me in the back my first Sunday and each Sunday afterward, since no other church members ever strayed to the black corner. In fact the row directly in front of ours was always the last to be occupied and remained empty if other places available. Which they increasingly were, as newer denominations attracted membership and the good reverend Parker's droning taught *stay away, stay away* each Sunday.

With such a meager and docile band of Africans, content to cling meekly to the bottom rung of the church, I often wondered why Parker felt obliged to spice his anecdotes of religious extravagance always it seemed with Negro characters. For example, the slave Caesar exhorting a motley crowd then attempting to lie with an Indian woman who'd listened to his preaching, telling her to entice her to commit lewdness with him that Hell was not so dreadful a place as had been described by the parish priest's sermon, nor was it so difficult to enter Heaven as the priest had set forth. The reverend Parker smirking as he listed lads and boys, yes, women and girls, yes, and oh yes, Negroes among those who have taken it upon themselves to do the business of preachers. Was he concerned about the spiritual well-being of our dusky corner of St. Matthew's when he warned that black people especially were susceptible to revival preaching. That we were exceedingly wrought upon in an uncommon manner that set us to crying out, swooning, dancing, groaning, disrupting the proper business of church, not only making fools of ourselves, but dangerous fools.

Were his remarks addressed with loving concern to us. If not, whom was he warning. Why did Parker expend so much of his precious time castigating us, calling attention to us with a recital of the alleged misdeeds of our brethren, we who were so few, so ignored, unsupported and unwelcome as to be invisible in every other aspect of the church's affairs.

After services concluded, I would tarry awhile with the African families. A dozen or so of us, young, old, hale and crippled, destitute, thriving, would walk a ways together, along the main thoroughfare out of the village, eastward where the modest farms and households of black folk lay.

Soon after my arrival in the vicinity I had constructed a brush arbor, off the main road, at the end of a common pasture crossed by a tolerable footpath. In a clearing screened by trees, not many steps beyond the point where pasture ended and woods began, we would worship again at this humble arbor. Simple worship of prayers and song, a short scripture I would read and render, testimony from any or all who felt the call.

Perhaps it was the long drought of St. Matthew's that made the singing sweet as cool water after great thirst. Even my poor voice grew wings when it soared with the others. We filled that grove with song. Yes we did. Cathedralized it. As I think back on those Sunday mornings, I hear music in everything. In the unhurried cadence of our stroll to the arbor, in the sacred rhythms of scripture, in the tales we told one another we called prayer and witness, in the casual chatter, news and laughter we exchanged after the meeting broke up. Yes, music even in the silence. The long, silent distance between this land and home, recalled in breaks between choruses, in the quiet when an anthem ended.

The singing is over. Quiet descends. Large, large, falling on us like rain. A soaking stillness while the singing floats off somewhere else. Up through the leaves. A transparent cloud, soundless and emptied. In this quiet I hear the birds again. One or two, then many. Many, many unseen in the woods. Someone who didn't understand might have thought the trees had voices. Chirping, cawing at one another. The forest talking to itself.

I often wondered if the birds stopped their chattering while we sang our hymns. Sometimes you couldn't hear your own voice in the swell of everyone else's. How could you hear the silence of the birds, if it was there, waiting for you to finish.

Did the birds listen to us sing. Heaven listen. How would you ever know. Were the winged creatures curious. Outraged. Why is this motley crew of blackbirds invading our grove, drowning our songs. Could the birds learn our hymns. Add verses.

People talking now. You can listen to the conversations or you can listen to the birds. Not both at once.

Mr. Rowe is a crooked house with legs. His broad back hides his neighbors from my view as he limps from one group to another, shaking hands, bestowing God speeds and God blesses. His thundering bass the foundation rock of our harmonies. Our drum.

Beautiful service, he booms. And Got gib one fine day for it.

Amen. Amen, Brother Rowe.

I remember him smiling. Gazing up through the shaggy trees at the blue sky. What did Rowe see. He had run away from slavery with a wife and four small children. Only he survived the flight north. One of his huge hands had been mutilated by paddyrollers. When he shook yours, the two remaining fingers on the nub closed round your hand like a grappling hook. Some of his toes lopped off. They said the plowed skin of his back rough as oak bark. His whole dark body a map of torture. How could he smile. What did he see. Worshiping with him and the other Africans who gathered in the clearing was teaching me to be curious in new ways. Ask new questions about them, about myself.

Weekly communion with a band of fellow Africans was a novel experience for me. I'd been born on an isolated farm. My mother, brother and I were slaves in a district of modest holdings. Except for my two masters, no one in the neighborhood owned Negroes.

Confined as we were by geography and situation, as a boy I seldom saw any new faces, let alone black ones like mine.

You smile. Yes. I understand. You see before you a brightish mulatto man calling himself black. A silliness, I agree. I wish the memories associated with this usage evoked only smiles.

No other faces, then, of "African-descended people." I must have been eight or so when I saw my first truly dark man. I'm sure my mouth dropped open. It's quite possible I gasped.

I labor this point in order to remind you of another. I had not yet been to Philadelphia. Plague had not cast the city's shadow over those of us who lived beyond the city's boundaries. The simple joy of meeting each Sunday with the black people (many shades, yes, yes) of Radnor was not prompted by any negative predisposition toward whites (yes, also many shades).

The Bible had been my teacher. Its lessons confirmed my experience up to this sojourn at Radnor. My first master a devil incarnate, but the second a benevolent man. He'd allowed himself to be persuaded by his saintly wife to make Christians of his slaves. She taught my brother and me to read the Bible. For which privilege I shall forever be grateful. As I am eternally grateful to this same master for permitting my brother and myself to hire ourselves out and purchase our mother's freedom, then our own.

I was kindly used by my Quaker family, though I was their property, their captive, their thing by law. Their specific kindnesses made it impossible for me to condemn generally the white race. Despite the memories of a brutal master's abuse of my mother, despite the evil of bondage blighting my prospects, despite the humiliation of separation in God's house. Furthermore, until I was a strapping lad of eleven or so, most people I saw, good or bad, were white. So I believed what I read in the Bible. All men equal in God's sight. That precept guided my practice. Sin had leveled all mankind. Salvation through God's mercy, obedience to His law, the only means by which any of us might rise.

After I'd discovered my vocation, I would preach wherever willing ears would listen. Dark faces seldom appeared at the doors of farmhouses, on village greens, at markets or fairs, weddings or funerals, the churches, meeting halls and taverns where I sought to spread God's word, the saving grace of the inner light. The few dark faces I did encounter quickly faded, just as white faces blended one into another, because I stayed constantly on the move.

Steady employment with Stubbs altered my circumstances. Still I did not choose the people of my little flock at Radnor because of their color. I did not force them to cluster at the rear of St. Matthew's. I did not design nor did I preside over a service each Sunday in the church that insulted, excluded and mocked the heartfelt desires of the colored folk to worship God with body and soul. No. It was St. Matthew's that rebuked and scorned them. Set them apart. When these circumstances became clear to me, I felt it my Christian duty to convey God's word to the strait place where black folk were stranded, the neediest of the needy. My invitation, even so, was general. Whites were always welcome to join us as we walked to our humble brush arbor. I was young enough, innocent enough, to be surprised none did.

Before Mr. Rowe and most of the others were swept off the face of the earth in a single night of horror, my curiosity finally got the best of me. I took old Rowe aside one afternoon and asked a question that had long puzzled me.

Your smile positively glows, Mr. Rowe. A smile like one of God's elect, my friend. Pray share with me the vision that beams in your face.

Since you ax me, Reverend, Ima tell you. I'm so happy you ax me, Reverend, cause ain't many peoples ever axt old Rowe why he smiling nor why he crying nor much of nothing, if truth be told, sir. You a preacher, Reverend, but you a good young fellow too so Ima tell you. Scuse me if I say something I ain't spozed to say, Reverend. This just a plain old nigger telling you the plain old truff like you ax me.

Sometime I looks at the sky and close my eyes I see the whole world startin over again. New day, Reverend. Clean. See a black man and a black woman and a white man and a white woman laid side by side fresh out of the oven and theys the only people God done made.

Black man he wake up first this time. Remember everything. Quick. Grab ax. Chop white man head.

Then it the first black man and he butt naked and reared over the first white woman and she butt naked too with her legs cocked wide open and that thang down there wide open snapping up to get him like a blue-gum turtle but the black man he got this plug of mud he sticks up in there first. Shoves it way up. Then the boy give her a good ramming. Hammers that plug up so far and tight it ain't never coming out and she ain't never gonna push out no white babies so ain't gone be no more white peoples cept this one woman and he fixing her up good won't have to worry with her no more neither. And he's smiling whilst he's ramming. And that, scuse me, Reverend, what I see sometimes when you see me smiling up at Heaven. Amen.

A Sunday in October. I sit with the others on our bench at the rear of St. Matthew's. With apologies to the Lord, my mind's wandering as usual while Parker discourses, as absent from St. Matthew's in his daydreaming as I am in mine. I revive myself by anticipating our second worship in the clearing, recite the verse I've chosen for the meeting later in the day, Jeremiah 5:14. *Behold, I am making my words in your mouth a fire, and this people wood, and the fire shall devour them.*

For an instant two daydreams collide. A tongue of flame shot from Parker's lips. In his collar and cross, his black, lank-winged coat, could he prophesy. Could the Holy Spirit possess him. Could he utter strange words stabbing us to our hearts. His voice a bull's bellow, a mighty trumpet.

Only for an instant and only in my imaginings did flames erupt from Parker's lips, his shrill voice thunder. A silly notion. Entertaining myself so I don't fall asleep while Parker drones. Words in his mouth mumbled ashes.

Yet who knew how the Lord chose his messengers. How would you know you were the one anointed to bear God's good news, the scourging, hungry news that strips flesh from bone, turns bone to dust. Makes whole nations quake. Why couldn't this hair-splitting, chilly priest be a messenger. Was that notion any more preposterous than thinking myself, unschooled, black, poor, a proper vessel to bear truth and prophecy.

My musings suddenly interrupted by the earthshaking *tramp tramp* of a giant beast. A hideous dragon, red-eyed, scaly, lumbering toward the church. The earth gouged by its taloned feet. Field and forest leveled to blackened cinders by its fiery breath. A saddle on the hillock of its humped back. What rider could mount this steed. Who but Death spur it through the countryside, smashing villages and towns, laying waste this sinful land, preparing it for the Savior's coming.

✣

He hears the beast striding closer. The rough planks of the floor quiver. The creature's looming shadow blots bright day from the windows. From its cavernous mouth, its flaring nostrils, flames crackle. They are cold lights flashing round his head. In the only glance he can spare before the storm of lights blinds him, he glimpses the row of dark faces, the fence of stringy-haired skulls separating them from the pulpit.

She almost appears, but it's not time yet. Not quite yet.

St. Matthew's wooden walls turn down like Jericho's walls of stone, like pages of a book, opening upon a fantastical landscape. He could see as far as the ends of the earth in every direction. All the fabled scenes he'd ever imagined were accessible to him. Mist-crowned mountains of jade, a blue-black ocean in which craggy fields of ice float, an ancient Hindu temple, a marble city girding seven hills. Mosques, minarets, a desert littered with white bones, jungles teeming with shy, ferocious creatures, a city with rivers for streets, the peaked tents of wild Indians, a garden of luxurious plants whose smiling human faces hang upside down. The world, its far-flung wonders, contracted so everything could be encompassed by his vision. This world and a multitude of others whose existence had been hidden until the walls of the church fell away and he found himself seated at the center of a disc upon which the universe was shrunken and arrayed. Nay, not shrunken. There was no diminishment of scale or distance. Better, its immensity rendered available. The miracle was that near and far had become interchangeable. Things close at hand, things separated from him by a continent, were blended. One. He roamed everywhere at once. At any moment exactly where he needed to be.

Instead of being overwhelmed by the infinite vistas, he was

flooded by peace. The world rotated around him, rapidly at its farthest edges, imperceptibly in the lazy, glowing space at the center where he was poised. First chance, he'd tell the others — when all your desires are granted, you have no desires.

But he had no wish yet to say anything to anyone. He was all the others. They were thinking with his thoughts. Their thoughts were his. He lived uncountable lives. Breathed for all of them, dying and being born so quickly life never started or ended. It flowed. One continuous sweet breath, just as his vision never alighted on one object, one place, but danced to them, through them, so he missed nothing but nothing halted his gaze either and the world was one sight, one luminous presence inventing his eyes.

The vision lasted no more than a second. Not long enough to contain this thought: what I'm seeing is a foretaste of that wondrous clarity arriving only after a fainting fit has smashed me down. I'm falling. Ponderously. Slowly falling toward the oblivion of a fit. The many worlds compressed in this vision dissolving. Gone already. A fit's coming here in the Church of St. Matthew where I sit with my African brethren. They will share my shame. Smothering calm rendering me mute before I can utter a word of warning to them.

The universe kneels, retreats through the needle's eye. Whence it came. The gaping portals of St. Matthew's collapsed walls snap shut. He's hurled against the towering ramparts of a city. Lies curled against dank stones. Of the great city beyond the walls he could hear and see nothing. He's shivering. Someone is weeping uncontrollably. Gradually, as he becomes aware of hard ground, a hard wall, cold, dark shadows enclosing him, he understands he is the one crying.

For a time he lay unmoving. Time without beginning or end. In weather unchanging, a wet, dismal spring morning while traffic in and out of the city's eye passed by him as if he were invisible. Lost and found. Found and lost. His tears dry up. The pity he feels for himself cracks. He grows weary of asking himself why anyone would want to be the abandoned creature he is and still wish to live. He lacks energy for questions. Exhaustion smothers all questions, all answers. He's been locked in an invisible cage bolted to a rock too long to remember how long or why or care.

First flashing lights. Then this numbness and immobility. Like death. Except the candle not quite snuffed. One last pinpoint throwing no light or heat. Too weak to do anything more than remind him, in the faintest of whispers, life's not over yet. Your punishment for bad faith is to lie forever on this forlorn shore waiting for a wind to rise, a merciful breath that will fill the drooping sails shrouding your shoulders or extinguish the last pitiful spark of light.

He hears a commotion. Sees many feet. Many sorts of shoes. They speak to him. Shoes have tongues. They do do do. And sly voices. A heel and sole smeared with cow dung. Peeking from beneath the hem of a petticoat a woman's narrow, tapered boot. Inside her silk stockings her naked toes like piglets stacked at a sow's teats. Frayed laces. A silver buckle. Little shoes. Big shoes. Scuffed. Polished. Torn. A plump, linen-stockinged calf. Breeches. Shoes. Shoes. Shoes. An ark of shoes, two by two.

How dare you. How dare you. Get him up and out of the church. This instant. Up and out, I say.

Spaces between the preacher's words. Within the words. Long pauses no one else seems to notice. Each word breaking apart. Necklaces of sounds unstrung, beads slipping off the wire, ping-ing, clicking, tapping, rolling on the floor around him. Why doesn't anyone stoop to catch them.

I won't allow it. An abomination. Who is this madman. Up with him. Out. Out.

How long had he been cowering on the floor of St. Matthew's. His screeches and foul oaths the most passionate preaching ever heard within these walls. Are his breeches wet. Is he frothing at the mouth like a mad dog. If he growls, will the crowd scurry away. On all fours he lopes after reverend Parker, nipping his surly coattails, howling, a hound from Hell driving him from the temple.

An uncontrollable urge to laugh. To laugh and laugh and laugh. An irresistible, rollicking laugh. The congregation will tumble down around him, laughing, rolling, holding their bellies, laughing so hard it hurts.

His cheeks are flooded with salty tears. It only felt for a moment like laughter. This trembling and dizziness. These giddy secrets he aches to share.

A parliament of shoes on the planks. I am your prime minister. The king's tongue.

He gags. His policy a nasty gruel of slop consumed yesterday. Leftover porridge splashed in the barnyard for the pigs.

Oink. Oink. Thank you, prime minister. Thank you, sir.

They shake shoes off their cloven hooves. Hooves sharp as axes. They trample him, his head part first. Mercifully, he won't have to watch the rest of his body chopped to bloody bits.

Lord have mercy. He's coming round. Thank you, Jesus. My, my, my. Is he all right. Poor child. God's bringing him through. He be fine. Praise Got. His eyes opening. You-all give him room to breathe, sisters.

You can imagine what they're saying, the dozen or so good souls keeping watch as I stirred, then gradually revived. They'd laid me on a bed of grass, someone's shawl or coat pillowing my head. My mouth wiped clean and dry. My clothes — they told me later I'd been trying to tear them off my body — rearranged, refastened. The women had already decided who'd feed me, board me, nurse me, which of them would mend the rents in my shirt. Somehow, as if their good intentions had been carried out, I was awakening whole and healed.

A rim of brown faces and above them a green ring of treetops silhouetted against bright sky. I couldn't pick out faces. Just blurry arcs of brown, green, a bluish silver lid. The voices belong to anyone, everyone, anonymous as the hidden birds who'd made the woods seem to speak. Some Sundays when our singing was best, the clearing sounded like Heaven might sound. Sheltered within a hovering band of dark angels as I was that October afternoon, is that how Heaven might feel.

I wondered how I'd been transported from St. Matthew's to the brush arbor. It was the first question I remember asking out loud. According to them the question was not my first. My first words in the clearing, my eyes still shut, they said, were Bible words, the verse from Jeremiah. *Behold, I am making my words in your mouth a fire . . .*

Since I returned to this world with God's words on my lips, they thought God had touched me. Laid me low in the dungeon so I might receive His word and prophesy. When I awakened speaking scripture I frightened them, some told me later. They believed I was delivering God's judgment upon them. You didn't sound like you, they said. Still a little wild, a stranger dropped amongst them.

Old Mr. Stevens said he thought I was a goner. Them devils had you in the church. They all up inside you. Had you jumping juba on them floorboards. Like to turn you inside out, son.

If them pepper and brimstone devils don't finish you, Mr. Scant-gut-scarecrow hisself, Ole Nick-in-disguise Parker, at the head the queue waiting his turn.

My, my. Never seen such commotion over one poor colored boy. Church finished lickety-split soon's you hit the floor hollering. Yes indeed. Some them run way. Rest behind Parker huffing down the aisle to get you.

You didn't pay them no mind. Uh-uh. You just keep on kicking and rolling about and shaking and crying till you wore your ownself out. Parker couldn't do nothing but fuss. They shooed the womens and childrens. Don't know what the men woulda done to you iffen some us don't stand right close by your side.

Tell the truth, I had no idea what to do with you neither, son. Never seen nothing like it. Smoke coming out your ears and nose. Yes indeed. You was a sight.

Musta worn yourself out. Or them debils wore theyselves out whippen on you cause you just lay there quiet afterwhile. Eyes all rolled back up in your head.

Rowe, he pick you up then. Slung you over his shoulder like a sack of cornmeal. Tote you outside.

Somebody said the best thing to do be what we always do Sunday. G'wan down to de arbor.

My African brethren believed I was touched by something not of this world. And I was. But not in a manner anyone need fear. The fits I suffer produce no supernatural powers, no tongue of flame. Only a sweet, brief clarity.

Sure enough, a vision did enrapture me while I lay recovering in the clearing. But I couldn't share it. The clarity touches me, then passes swiftly. I can't teach it to stay. Nor do I have words to convey a thousandth part of what I glimpse, the truth of this world rushing back through the pinhole that swallows it when the black fits seize me.

A rush. Then the absolute peace of knowing the world's whole again. The infinite parts miraculously reassembled. In an instant. Seamlessly.

Amen. I breathe a kind of amen to myself again and again. Say it aloud, softly. *Amen.*

I wish I could share it. I wish someone else, one of my friends in the clearing, anyone, could read the glad tidings in my eyes. See how each separate, lonely thing connects for an instance with its lost brethren. As in a mirror my eye finds my eye. Or as in another's gaze I find my self. The play back and forth. A simple fellowship, each freeing the other, making the other real.

She appears as soothing coolness. Water from somewhere someone carried to the clearing. A handkerchief soaked in cool water wipes my forehead. I am sitting in the grass. As upright as I dare. A moment before, I'd been steady enough to navigate the stars. Now I don't risk standing. With my eyes closed, nothing had been hidden from me. No secrets I needed to know eluded me. Now, regaining my senses in the familiar clearing, I am blinded by the ordinary light of an October afternoon.

I feel giddy again, as I did on the floor of St. Matthew's. A child again. Tangled in the consequences of some dumb thing I've done, helpless till my mother's smile, her patience, undoes the mess I've made for myself. Honey stuck in my nappy hair. A wasp stinger hooked in my thumb. The pail of milk I tripped over and spilled, running, after I'd been instructed a thousand times *walk, walk, walk, boy.*

Water cool and healing on my brow as my mother's hand. A touch that familiar, that far away. Someone tending me, a fragrance, a blue rustling in the air. Sleeves the color of sky passing back and forth close to my face.

Voices continue to discuss me as if I'm not there. I can assign faces to speakers though I can't see anyone yet. I say their names to let people know I'm returning.

Hello, Rowe. Thank you, Mrs. Lewis. God bless you, Sister Jones. Thank you, Cudjo.

She moves off, a blur in the corner of my eye, to join the other folk huddling round me. A bluish shadow slipping into the circle, invisible behind the others by the time I turned in her direction.

My eyes continue to deceive me. A reluctance to quit the feast of clear-seeing. Old Stevens was right. Fighting the devils had exhausted me. Not only my eyes, my entire body resists the work of making ordinary sense of things.

Why couldn't I find her. Why did the clearing seem so crowded. People everywhere. People in outlandish costumes. Shoes from my dreams. A bazaar of people milling about. More African people than I'd ever seen in one place at one time. A throng far too numerous to be contained in the small space of the brush arbor. Different faces, groups differently appareled in each direction I scan. Replaced by newcomers if I glance away and then back at the same spot. Swarms of people drifting, shuttling, filling the clearing.

My familiar brethren seem not to notice the mob engulfing them. They remain clustered round me. When Mistress Jones detaches herself from the group and leads young Lucy by the hand toward the woods, they pass through the airy presence of the visitors like pebbles through reflections on water.

Was the young woman in the blue dress who'd bathed my brow one of us or one of the others. I knew everything and nothing about her. I was certain she was young, certain she was a woman. Certain of the color of her dress. Her scent. Though I'd not seen her face, I was positive she'd not worshiped with us previously. She could be a stranger and still belong with us. The faces in our little congregation weren't the same every Sunday. For various reasons not everyone attended regularly. Visitors tried us. Some came once, never returned. A handful you could count on, but even among this faithful few, illness or accident or weather or worse could prevent attendance. The rural life was hard. Limited by the sparse number of Africans within the vicinity, our tiny band waxed and waned each Sunday.

Was she a visitor. A dependent who'd recently joined one of the regular families. Or was she kin to the myriad others I see whether my eyes closed or open as I sit, dazed, drained by the effort of recovering my wits.

Thusly I met her the first time. Thusly she returns. The more I've thought on it since, the more I wonder if she belonged, like those other presences crowding the arbor that day, to the world of special seeing.

In the clearing I witnessed two roads crossing. One for people like us, who worshiped at St. Matthew's. The other a thoroughfare frequented by our ancestors, our generations yet to be born. One highway solid earth, the other air, the stuff of the invisible ether where angels float. Perhaps seeing the spirit road and those who traverse it meant I was on my way to join them. The falling fit my middle passage. But she crossed over instead. Tended me. And perhaps because she tarried a moment to cool my feverish brow, perhaps she was left behind. If not left behind, suspended between her world and ours.

Yet I swear to you, the touch, the coolness, were real. The fragrant blue cloud of her gown rustling, enfolding me, was real.

Fancy carries me away. Of course she was a flesh-and-blood woman. I asked after her for weeks. Months. In the excitement and confusion of my fainting and its aftermath, no one in our group remembered her. From the scanty particulars of my description how could anyone identify her. Yes. No. Maybe. Blue? Perfume? A traveler on her way somewhere else who happened by, chancing upon a caravan of black folk in their Sunday best, on an October Sunday, one of their own slung over a giant's shoulder. Who wouldn't stop and stare at the sight.

She follows the procession when it turns off the main road, onto a footpath overgrown with the tall, dry grass of that season. Follows us into the thick woods, to our humble threshing ground. Watches Rowe lay me down. Struck by his size, strength, the deftness of his broken hands. Who are these African people, she asks herself. Is this a funeral. Some pagan rite of our forefathers preserved in this new land.

One of them places a rolled shawl under the prostrate man's head. They surround him, heads bowed. A murmuring like bees. What do they intend, hiding themselves away deep in this grove of trees. Surely no bloody sacrifice of one of their own kind. No savage cries or dancing. No. They are bright-eyed children, dignified men and serious matrons. Her people in a somber, concerned mood. Yet agitated, alarmed.

No birdsong in the clearing. All nature hushed, expectant. She realizes she too is holding her breath.

The young man bolts up to a sitting position. His words are fire. The wall of black people shies away from his voice. The fire gallops, leaps over the trees, a ball of flame streaking somewhere.

It's over quickly. The man shudders once. Rests quietly after his utterance. Fire on its way to do its work. Warn the people. A burning house glows orange behind dark hills. He settles back on his arms. They are talking to him. Comforting, soothing, gentle words. Prayers. Blessings.

Where she finds water he can't say. Can't account for the miracle of its coolness. But she surely does find it and surely wipes his forehead. He knows her face only from inside out. As if he's slipped into the quiet chamber inside her skull where she sits and looks out at him. He would never forget the feel of being in that room. It is what he knows best of her. Her way of peering out at him, from the throne behind her eyes, eyes he can't even say for sure the color of.

This enterprise, this speaking into the dark as if it would raise you from the dead. Why am I driven to it. Why don't I lie down beside you. Sleep your sleep. Why the whispering in your cold ear — words, words, words, as if silence isn't enough. Silence our proper meeting place.

She once complained that my stories are too unhappy. If you wish to cure me, she said, why all these tales drawing down the corners of my mouth. Cheer me, sir. I'm acquainted all too well with the vale of tears your stories inhabit.

I took up her challenge. Searched my mind for a story with a happy ending. But being who I am, being locked in this struggle to cure her, a struggle whose outcome grows less certain with each passing day, the best I could offer was the story of my stay with the couple who had rescued me from the storm, a happy beginning at least, hoping to divert her, keep her listening till she provided the only possible happy conclusion to any story I might recount. Till she returned from wherever she'd gone, escaped from whatever was dragging her down.

Tea, sir. Hot tea.

Was it her voice. Had he found the gate again, died and entered it again.

He is cold. Too cold to shiver. He needs to shiver, loosen the cold's grip. He's a lump of something cold and unmoving. Bedclothes heaped over him. Heavy with the reek of strangers' bodies, their heat, sweat soaked into the covers, but nothing penetrates to warm him. If his frozen limbs move, they'll shatter.

She's speaking to him again. Words he can't sort out, the voice dimly familiar. He wants to respond. Open his eyes. He tries and hears ice splintering or bones snapping. A sizzling pain rummages through him. He promises the pain he'll never try to stir again if only this once *please please please* it goes away and leaves him in peace.

They had been huge and beautiful. White butterflies, feathers, petals, scraps of the purest foolscap floating down. Their fall so slow and stately you could follow the career of each one, appreciate how each differed in shape from the others. No wind deflected them. Occasionally one drifted slightly or twisted or tumbled from the strict drill to obey its own peculiar nature. Huge white particles hanging in the air, catching the light, transforming it. Something dropping from the sky that requires a name not spoken before.

At first the big moist drops blotted on his clothes. Disappeared immediately. Then the wind rose, howling, swirling. He's crusted head to foot with white. Snow whips and roils, blinding him, bowing him, needles of snow, slanting walls of snow, snow cascading in avalanches off the trees.

Cold numbs his feet first. Near the end, until his mind's too tired to play the game, he keeps himself awake by picturing a man trudging through a blazing desert. If he keeps the little sweaty figure moving across the landscape of dunes and dust devils and sweltering drafts, he believes his actual body, of which he feels nothing, won't succumb to the cold. He could be walking, crawling or sitting in the snow. No clues from his body. Only snow, wind, aching numbness, the howl of the blizzard. His thoughts race, then they stumble, collapse in a muddled heap. The thought of pitying himself, the thought of blaming himself, the thought of laughing at himself. The thought he may be perishing, or already dead, the thought he may survive if he keeps walking. The thought that he has no way of telling which thought makes sense of his circumstances.

The storm dropped him at our door. I don't recall why I decided to open it. Probably to see if a world beyond our door still existed. I was suspicious. Couldn't believe something so wild and threatening, so powerful it had lifted the house in its fist, rattled it like dice — I didn't think the storm could just go away as suddenly as it had arrived, leave no sign of itself behind except utter stillness, a landscape soft, rounded, stretched serenely as the body of a woman sleeping in the moonlight when I had crept to the window, lifted the shutter and peeked out.

Suspicious the storm was still lurking about, waiting to pounce if I let down my guard. Suspicious it may have snatched the world away, left the house standing to mark the emptiness. Had the storm truly passed, truly spared us and the sparing no cruel joke.

When I opened the door, my way was blocked by a wall of snow as high as my knees, planed flat where it had drifted against the door's bottom. I would not have ventured further except there, barely ten paces distant, a hulking tombstone had been planted in the front yard.

It was a huddled figure covered with snow. A frozen man who'd crawled as far as he could before strength had deserted him, safety only a few steps away.

Had he been drawn like a moth by our flickering lights. Or by smoke from the chimney. Or had he wandered snowblind until chance felled him this cruelly close to aid. Could he have been outside as we prepared for bed, him unable to move or make a sound we'd hear above the storm's racket. He might have seen the window go dark after I closed the shutter, extinguished a candle. Thinking of a man stranded in the snow, dying alone in the night, I should have pitied him the miserable ending of his life. I did, but I also resented him for sneaking up on us in the dark. I didn't like the idea of him observing us, asking himself what we might be doing, who we might be. Us unaware the whole time of his existence. Him hungrily aware of ours. Entwined with him, forced to share the intimacy of his last moments on earth.

He'd contracted himself into the smallest possible space, thighs pulled to his chest, head slumped forward against his knees, hoarding the last warmth in the cave of his folded body.

I didn't consider the possibility he might be alive. Took my time plowing through the snow to reach him. A noise like a grunt when I began to bat away the snow. I was more careful then. Worked to free his face from the rag muffling it. Whiskers of ice. Frozen breath, spit, tears, snot. More color in his skin than I'd expected. My African color. Had he crossed an ocean to find his icy death.

A hint of sun in his skin, so I pursued the slim chance his insides might retain a spark of the sun's heat. In this instance, at least, his color his salvation.

I couldn't tell much by touching. My bare hands numb in the frigid air. I push back his head. Lean over him. My breath's a steamy cloud. From the cracked black wound of his lips, nothing. I pry his mouth open, press the backs of my hands against his cheeks. Blow. Chafe. Rest my lips on his skin. But I'm not sure. My eye is almost touching his mouth. I wait for a breath to graze my lashes.

One comes. Another . . . then I'm sure. I work harder, faster. Knock off crusted snow. Rub bare skin. The man's body is dead weight. I get my hands up under his armpits. Start backing through the track I'd dug just minutes before, drag the man behind me to the house.

She'd been asleep when I got up, but I call through the door anyway. *He's alive. This dead man's alive.* In the fresh covering of snow, his heaviest part smooths a track, like a trowel pointing mortar between rows of bricks.

In front of the fire I strip him. He's unsteady as a drunk. I must prop him up while I pull off his clothes. Slippery puddles of melting snow spot the floor. His clothes are stiff as bark. I can't be certain skin's not coming off with the layers I peel. Too close and the blaze in the fireplace will roast the man's skin. Too far and the fire will do him little good. Can't turn him like a chicken on a spit so I wrap him in a blanket, and we stagger to the bed.

Undress.

I wait till she is naked under the covers. Pull the blanket off the man's shoulders, raise the covers, guide him down to drop alongside her. Quickly I remove my own clothes and crawl into the bed. She's lying on her stomach, her arm the only part touching him. Rigid as a fence. I reach across the man. Nudge her up, pull her toward me. We grasp one another, arms over and under the man, drawing closer together, holding on, embracing the cold presence between us.

Sometime before dawn a shivering awakens her. She's been shivered to sleep. Now she's shivering awake. She recalls how her flesh trembled when the warmest parts of her — bosom, belly — were forced to make contact with the frozen man. Broken sleep, restless dreaming. The man's shudders, his moans like the creeks and rivers in the mountains each spring twisting out of winter's grip. Raped by cold. Her body violated by the man's icy flesh pushing into private spaces. Violence and pain. Assaulted in her bed, losing herself, ripped away from the peace of sleep by his urgent need, its quaking hunger, her own helpless, shivering rage.

She reaches below the bedclothes into a tangle of limbs. In spite of fireglow, this corner of the room dark. Darker where her hand gropes. *Undress*, he'd hissed, and she'd obeyed. She's naked and cold now. So much cold in the stranger's body it had sucked the heat from her. Instead of saving this stranger's life, were they losing theirs. Precious heat leached from their blood. Three carcasses the animals will discover when the season changes, thawing bodies start to stink.

It must have been her leg, the coldest part of her, that pried her awake. Squeezed under the weight of other limbs, her leg had been sweating. Sweat turning to icy fingers on her thigh when, still half asleep, she'd freed it. She shifts again. Drapes her chilly leg over someone else's.

Undress. The only word she'd heard. A low, hissing whisper in Liam's throat. Loud enough to startle her from sleep. Alert her to sounds in the darkness above her head — shuffles, grunts and groaning. More than one person, she was sure. Rustle of clothing and bedclothes. Her whole being shrinking from the brunt of a sudden frigid draft. Thud of a body striking the bed. She shudders when she grazes ice-cold flesh. The bump and push of more scrambling weight in the bed. Hands grasping her shoulders. Fire and ice. Hands turning her, pulling her onto a slab of ice and fire.

A stranger's naked legs in the darkness beneath the covers now. Two legs not unlike the legs she's slept beside so many years she's stopped counting. Liam on top of her, beside her, behind her, his legs indistinguishable from hers when they had coupled, crawled, curled, wrestled all those nights. One animal with four legs they'd ridden till it dropped them here, this night, this bed, these two new legs strangely like Liam's but not his, the same and different. Younger legs. More meat on the thigh, a roundness of hip, but long-muscled like Liam's, flesh that will be stretched and stringy tough soon enough.

Hand her eyes now, reading the men. This stranger flat on his back, Liam beyond him, one arm flung across the man's chest as if he's still reaching for her in his sleep. Raising herself slightly, she leans over the man to rub Liam's back, the flap of a breast dragging across the man's chest. Her hand runs down the curve of knuckled spine to the split of Liam's narrow behind, a geography familiar as the map of her own face, then glides back up to the valley between the jutting bones of his shoulders. If flesh were the texture of snow, the heel of her hand would have left a trail like the one behind the body dragged inside the house. Her fingers walk the column of his neck, play in close-cropped fuzz, the bare skull above it.

The shape of Liam's body is an infant sleeping curled against the younger man's shoulder, bald head tucked under the other's chin. Liam's sound asleep. Snoring. Not a twitch when she touched him. She settles back down on the bed, shivering, burrowing deeper under the weight of bedclothes. Only the crown of her head uncovered, the spray of hair, black, black in the darkness, fanned on the pillow. Her bare skin, exposed a minute, feels as cold as the stranger's when she'd first touched him. But she'll warm up quickly. Wonders how long it took a body to become as cold as his. Wonders if he'll ever be warm again.

If you wore nothing but skin outdoors, would the moon's blue light warm you. If she kicked off the covers and ran naked into the snow, could she soak up moonlight, bring it back with her under the blankets where the men sprawled. Her flesh glowing in the dark. Moon-drenched, spreading the moon's pale blue heat.

She flops onto her back, nudges her haunch into the man's. In the cold air, her nipples had stiffened. She gently pinches and teases, awakening them again, hard and proud as they'd been when her breasts in their ripe glory. Nipples rising from breasts flat on her chest now, two ladles of batter spreading in a skillet.

The stranger doesn't stir when her fingertip finds a tiny bud on his chest, circles it, then its twin. His belly button is the secret, in-turning kind. She doesn't try to unlock it. Her hand slides lower. She rests against him to caress the shallow indentation, hard knob at its center, of Liam's hip.

The younger one's belly sleek. Not fat, not soft, firmly padded with a luxury of flesh age consumes. It could be Liam's body. Not his body today. One of those bodies stored in his she once could awaken and free. Surprises for both of them, their lovemaking a dance backward and forward in time.

The man's cheek almost touches Liam's. Liam's snoring, the sting of his breath seeps from another world. A world where he's become someone else, something else. Her smooth cheek shares the man's chest with Liam's bearded one. Has the whitish trail of spittle stained Liam's lip tonight.

She snuggles deeper. Her finger arcs slowly back and forth, from hipbone to hipbone, back and forth, following the curve of the man's belly, dip of his navel, the springy hair of his groin. She is remembering the look of surprise on Liam's face the first time she took him in her mouth.

The man's warm here. His little pot of boiling water. She pats the curly hairs. Swims her fingers through them, unkinking them, scratches the pebbly skin rooting them. She nudges his legs apart, making room for her hand to slide inside his thigh and follow the soft hair around to his buttocks. Twists her wrist and cups the pouch of wrinkled skin, raises it, palms its soft, dumb weight.

His legs spread wider. Shaft of his penis thickens. She rubs the saddled head of it, squeezing, rubbing. Traces its circumference with her finger, slowly in one direction, then another, around and back slowly, as she'd measured and primped her nipples, then his. Blood warms him, hardens him. She is a moon drawing the tide. It swells within her fist and she returns its pressure.

Will he die. When she lets go, will all the gathering heat spill out or will the creeks and streams and rivers inside him shunt warmth to every shivering corner.

When he's still again, she pushes up in the bed, arches her back, stretches her arm behind her and digs out her shift from under the pillow where she'd tucked it to keep it warm during the night. He'd started to tremble and she'd thought he'd surely awaken. Or surely die. She hadn't cared. If either man awakened or not. Lived or died. She had been smiling. Welcoming all and anyone, strangers, lovers, back to life. Herself to life. For a moment. For all the time there ever is.

As the last spasm had shaken him, his knees shot up. She hadn't let go till his legs relaxed, flopped down again on the bed. Now with her shift she mops his thigh, her leg, hand, dries a spot on the bed. When she finds Liam's knee, she discovers one more sticky drop. Scrolls it on a fingertip and raises it. Would it be hot or cold on her lips.

She hears Liam moving about the room. He's always up first. She listens to the noises of him trying to be quiet. She knows he wants her to sleep until she's ready to get up, but there is more to his quiet. Something secretive and driven, as if the rest of his day, the rest of his life, depends upon the hushed, unchanging tasks he performs each morning.

She follows the sounds of his routine. If someone asked her to recite the sequence the whole way through, she probably couldn't, or wouldn't, but she knows it the way she knows old songs she can't sing from beginning to end. Once they're started, whatever part she hears, she can sing the next line.

Old wood sighs. Poker breaking and spreading the last chunks. New logs crackle and hiss. Bark curls away, sparks pop from its blackened edges. The chair protests his weight as he sits down to pull on his boots. Water scooped and poured. Kettle's rattle and rusty sway as it's hung from the hook over the hearth. Does she really count his steps. *Three, four, five, six* to the window, time the silence after the shutter is lifted, fastened, and he gazes out *one . . . two . . . three . . .* Interval at the window exactly as predictable as the number of steps, the number of loose floorboards squeaking when he tiptoes from window to fireplace.

And so on and on, each sound she thinks seeking her as she awaits it. Church bells here in this blank wilderness tolling her awake each morning. Slight variations, themselves invariant, according to season, to weather. Is his job to obtain another day — for himself, for her, for the world — renewing a compact with powers that compel this daily repetition of duties.

He arranges their days, buys time for them, creeping about, opening a cupboard door, boiling water in the kettle, sitting down heavily at the table finally, as if the round of his obligations has exhausted him. Ten minutes drinking his tea — *can she hear him sip, hear tea trickle down his throat, splash into his belly* — then the chair will scrape away from the table, he'll execute the required number of steps to reach the door — *traps, he'll be checking the trapline this morning* — unlatch it, scuff it open and scuff it tightly shut behind him.

When he's gone she savors her morning aloneness, the vast emptiness of the bed, the expectant attentiveness of a day that's like a suitor to whom she hasn't quite said yes. She'll lie in bed a bit longer. Predictable herself now. So long a partner to the peculiar discipline of his days, her movements rhythmed to his whether he's actually there in front of her, leading the dance, or not. She enjoys the space of this house, uncluttered by him, relieved of his routine, though she fears her sense of freedom depends on him, the pattern he imposes on her days. These unbound moments grace notes worked into the iron composition securing them, binding them.

Some mornings she waits for him to return to bed. She can't help herself. She thinks such a return happened once and will happen again. She needs to believe the memory of him, bursting through the door, pouncing on her. Both of them grinning like fools. Laughing out loud because what they're doing feels good and they can do it again, anytime they please. And it's sad to have forgotten they can do it, forgotten how easy it is, but it's almost worth the wait, realizing again this sweet power they have over their lives, what they can do for each other if they step over a line. Take back what they've misplaced, neglected, themselves, how good they feel when they are these other people they still can be, will be the morning he hurries back to her.

Waiting for him, wondering why the memory of his return is elusive. If it ever happened. And if it didn't, why is she still waiting. A predictable, short-lived wait, because each morning her patience is defeated. Patterned like everything else.

Who is this, then. Sleeping like a baby. Skin less brown than Liam's. The back more deeply grooved. Same jutting shoulder bones. Had she fallen asleep waiting. Had she missed the noises of Liam returning. Did she remember what those noises would be. In their rhythms, their routine, was there still room for the sweet burst of him. She stares. Remembers this young man is a stranger. She's curious, but afraid to touch him. Is he alive.

After cleaning him, she'd dropped her shift on the floor. Now she fishes for it. Her hand closes on a stiff, wadded bit. She slips the shift over her head anyway. Quickly she's up, bare feet slapping the cold floor, toes feeling for her furry moccasins. She shivers. The dark, bunched stain on one edge of the shift scrapes against her leg. She hears Liam at the door. Shrugs a gown over the shift. Wonders why this morning of all mornings he's returned. She's not alone, not prepared for him. And this is the morning he picks.

She stands, her back close to the fire. Flips up the tail of gown, shift, fans heat on her legs. He won't look at her. A shy guiltiness in his eyes when he pushes back the hood of his parka. Cold clings to him, in his beard, on his eyebrows, the little extra noises of his clothes.

The traps. Your morning for the traps.

I started . . . but then I remembered the man.

Everything is fine. Go on and check your traps.

Thought you might be . . . frightened.

Afraid. Afraid of a cold, dead boy.

Dead. No. His heart beating . . . Better, he seemed better.

If alive is better, he's better.

A bad storm. I have to see to the animals. Then I remembered him. Here . . . don't know what kind of man he might . . .

Two-legged kind.

Didn't want to wake you. Or him.

I'm awake now. Fine now. He lived through the night and my guess is he'll live through the day. Many more days if he's meant to. Would you like more tea before you go out again. The water's hot.

He shakes his head.

He . . .

He stops after one word and regards her closely. As if gauging her response to unspoken words. His eyes dart away from her and dart back. His mouth falls open, then he compresses his lips to a fierce pout between mustache and bristling beard. A pause lasting long enough for many words to be uttered if only he could bring himself to say them. She's learned to treat these pauses as conversation. Extracts what she needs from the emptiness as he speaks less and less.

Should I see to him.

You go. To the animals. I'll see to him.

The hood swallows his bald head. Shaggy lining matches the mottled gray beard. She can tell how relieved he is to be on his way. For the routine to begin repairing itself.

Before he turns, he stares at her again, his lower jaw cranked forward, dark lips pursed, the lines of his face taut. Perhaps a *Thank you*, inaudible as it forms and fades.

Always a race. Pouring more hot water into the tub before what's already there gets cold. Enough to cover her hips, her ankles when she folds herself inside the barrel. Enough to take the chill out of the cask's bottom when she sits, enough to splash over herself so she's not shivering the whole time she washes. Enough so at least she feels cleaner when she stands and the draft punishes her while she dries herself. Easier with two doing the work of a bath. One in the tub, the other drawing, heating, pouring water. Liam helps her, lets her help him sometimes in the slot set aside for this chore. An end-of-fortnight, end-of-day chore. In the coldest months not worth the bother, he fusses. She'd brushed snow off the water barrel outside the door, cracked a thin skin of ice to fill the first pail this morning.

She steals baths. Steals precious water, precious time. Bathes in the squat cask he'd halved and sealed as a gift for her, her last luxury and vanity. A reminder of England, life in a great house in Liverpool. Her mistress's grand tub, a riot of painted scenes, carved cupids, satyrs and nymphs, a bench within upon which milady sat enthroned while servant girls bustled about warming towels at the cavernous fireplace, maintaining the steaming bathwater at the exact near-scalding temperature her ladyship demanded. Once, after her mistress, wrapped in towels head to foot, plump cheeks flushed scarlet, had been conveyed to the dressing room, she'd stayed behind, slipped off stockings and shoes, gathered petticoats, shift and gown in a bundle to her chin, stepped up on the alabaster stool and down into milady's tub, lowering herself waist-deep in a luxury of tepid water.

Now she must race to keep water warm around her hips, race to fit the whim of a bath into routines too grim and demanding to accommodate whims. She dips the stained edge of the shift into the tub. Quickly scrubs and rinses it. Drapes it on a stool drawn up to the fireplace. Then she steps into the ankle-deep water and sits, knees pulled to her chest, toes pushing one end of the cask, her back cut by the other.

Rapidly, she soaps and rinses. Is his spunk in the water with her. What did they look like, the tiny beings his spunk carried, little creatures too small for human eyes to see, swimming in her bathwater. Were there many or one. A miniature man or miniature woman nestled in an egg. An egg tiny as angels who could dance on the point of a pin.

Could an egg with its sealed, secret cargo live for long outside a body. How quickly would it need the shelter of a female's nest. Sleeping, resting, growing there. A single egg or an armada of eggs leaving one body, seeking another. One, it must be one. Why many if all but one must perish. One would suffice. Whether one or many, it would be a race. Always a race. To stay warm, to stay alive.

A race lost now. The water cooling as it laps between her thighs. Too late, now. Cold had killed them or killed *it* during the night. Even if some miracle had preserved the animicules in the stained gown, no warm place inside her. A chilly maze of caves and tunnels they'd drift through till they drowned.

Her gown on the hearth, beside the stool. A new warm skin for her day. One long step out of the tub, both hands on the rim to steady it, keep her balance at the awkward half-in, half-out moment when she pivots. At this exact, helpless moment she feels the stranger's eyes on her, on the hinge anchoring her outstretched leg.

Later he'll admit he'd been watching her the whole time. She didn't care. Long past the vanity of shame. She understood her old woman's body of little use or interest to anyone for anything. She was grateful for its hardiness. Hoped she could depend on it for the few years left her. She knew she'd once been beautiful to others. Any fool, even one as naive as she'd been, could read her beauty in men's eyes. The women's eyes staring when they thought she didn't see them appraising her. Women standoffish, afraid to look her in the eye because they couldn't hide their envy, their anger, their disappointment in themselves they tried to disguise as contempt of her. Youthful beauty had deserted her the way she'd heard mothers talk about being abandoned by the children they'd birthed and raised. Something inside her, part of her so long she'd forgotten that it possessed legs, a will of its own, until the day she discovered it gone.

She knew she'd been beautiful and knew it made no difference now. What kind of difference then. She seldom thought of that other, beautiful person. When she did, what she recalled mostly was trouble. Men's eyes nibbling her, spitting in her face what they chewed and couldn't swallow. Fear growing warts on the women's faces. If her body had not been beautiful, there wouldn't have been less trouble, just different trouble.

I open my eyes and I'm lost. Cold under a mound of covers in a strange bed. Dreamlike fragments fly at me too rapidly for me to hold on to anything except their rush, their urgency. Lost whether I open my eyes or keep them shut. I almost scream. Something tells me a scream might help, might be a beginning.

Then you. You beside the fire pulling off a gown, then a shift. I concentrate on this image of a woman I've never seen before, undressing in a house I don't remember entering. I'm weak and chilled and sick and hungry all at once. My head roaring. No. It's a fire. No, it's both, a roaring inside my skull and a roaring fire in the room. There is no difference. My skin gone. Sound strikes what skin is meant to shield. A layer under the skin, unused to sensation. What's in this room enters me. Cold. Fire noises. You. Your pale skin that doesn't quite fit. Pleated at knees, neck, tight at belly and breasts. I blink, but you're still there. Skin mottled, hair like fur in the firelight. The naked body beside the fire is my anchor. I blend the floating parts of you, slowly piece a world together.

You face me only a moment before you turn to the tub. Dip the shift you were wearing into it. You're bending over the tub, your arms extended, doing something I can't see with your hands and the shift. Why am I telling you all this. You know. You did it.

What I want to say is how odd I felt spying on a stranger, in that stranger's bed, in that stranger's house. How your body returned me to this world, your body familiar and ordinary as my own that morning. As unexpected and intimate.

I almost looked away. In your ill-fitting skin you were old enough to be my mother and like my mother you deserved your privacy. Except you weren't my mother so I watched.

When I was a child, my mother's body seemed mine. But I gave her back to herself, became ashamed to see her naked. Ashamed of myself for spying on her. Ashamed for her. Turning away from the dying stamped within her, working its way to the surface, changing her, taking her. Ashamed of losing her to this other I pretended not to see. The wrinkled other she couldn't help becoming.

An old woman undressing by the fire and I almost turned my head, but this time I wanted to see exactly what time costs. What it steals, what it leaves.

For all I knew I might be old, dying in a strange bed. Hopelessly muddled. Not a glimmer of what had occurred a moment before. An ancient invalid with no idea where I was. Who I was.

Then you began to change. Turning, twisting, leaning, bending. Arms over your head. A woman's motions, gestures old as time. Time evaporating like bathwater from your skin as you dry in front of the fire.

Perhaps I turned away an instant. Perhaps in that brief, brief absence, another woman, no, girl, took your place. A supple, smooth-fleshed girl toweling her freckled back. Raising her foot to dry between her toes. Muscles firm. Movements brisk. Her face unlined when she glances at the bed. Skin soft in the fireglow. As she hurries into her clothes, the black redness of her hair reflects fire. Fire catches color from her hair.

Was the room full of women. Women stepping into the cask, out of the cask. Each one different. Or changing. Different women, different ages. Magically transformed by water, fire, air.

You saw my eyes fixed on you when you stood at the foot of the bed. Waiting for you to tell me who I was. Where we were. You understood and smiled. A gracious smile dismissing my worries. The burden of my eyes. Your meaning clear. You told me I wasn't going to die. Said it without words and I believed you. You didn't say you'd saved my life, but I knew you were the one.

Tea, sir. Hot tea. Are you able to sit up and drink.

When he tries to move higher in the bed, he realizes his clothes are missing. With his arms beneath the covers he grips the top blanket to his chin, scoots slowly to a sitting position. His feet are blocks of ice. The blunt weight of them as he maneuvers sends throbbing pains into his legs. The message of the pain dull rather than sharp, informing him he's suffered a great injury and he's only beginning to understand its extent. He wants to kick his feet from under the covers and ask her to pour the tea on them. He thinks she'd do it if he asked. The thought makes him feel better. If he asked, would she fill the room with warm, soft petals floating down.

It's a bowl of tea. A bowl scooped from a block of wood. He takes it in both hands. The blanket slips from his shoulders. A plume of steam twists from the bowl's blackened center. He remembers the storm, his breath a web of brittle ice crumbling in his face. Gigantic snowflakes dropping in lines straight and precise as the dark, towering pines the king's agents once commandeered for the masts of ships. The white flakes never stop, they enter the ground and plummet through it, each one perfect, a shower of falling stars that pass into the blue-black ether buoying the earth.

You're just a boy. Do you speak, young fellow. Do you possess a name.

Like the tea, his name in his throat scalds him. He swallows, takes a deep breath, says his name again and it shocks him less, cooler this time, like the second sip of tea after he blows across the bowl's rim.

Her hands thick-veined, big-knuckled, bony. The skin papery and freckled, hands after she passes him the bowl of tea restless as a child's. Large hands he wishes she'd find occupation for, anything that might busy them so they don't dangle naked and awkward from the sleeves of her gown.

Hands attached to wrists attached to one of the women he'd been watching. Which one had stepped out of the tub into this skin, these hands, these shapeless layers of wool and linen.

Liam found you last night in the snow. More dead than alive, you were. Or perhaps you found us. Must have been an urgent errand to entice you abroad in such a storm. Storms are frequent and dangerous in this country. In this season. And the country sparsely settled. You must be new here.

He could explain he knew the country well enough, even though he'd not traveled this particular stretch before. Knew its bounties, its treacheries. A general knowledge earned by living upon the land, trekking alone like the hunters and trappers and Indians before him, who'd moved westward and northward deeper into the wilderness, into the mountains beyond these valleys and rolling hills, far beyond the fields that ax, saw and plow had cleared. But to know the country well was no guarantee you'd survive it. He could tell her he'd learned to treat this land with deep, abiding caution. The way deer bend to drink. And yet the skulls of deer litter the forest. He'd come by a route of his devising he'd never followed this far before, but the terrain had remained similar. His pace steady. He'd allotted more than sufficient time to reach the village of Radnor. The air was crisp when he began. A dour, low sky, negligible wind before noon. No sign of a blizzard.

He could say he hadn't been trying to outrun a storm nor pushing ahead foolishly into storm clouds massing on the horizon. He could explain how the storm abused him. Cunning, patient, invisible until it pounced full-blown upon his head. Sudden white flakes the size of oak leaves surrounding him. Too large to hold their shape, the snowflakes splashed silently on his skin, his clothes. By the time he tugged his cap from his pack, secured it under his chin with a strip of cloth, slants of snow had turned to fists of snow, a swirling melee. Whiteness everywhere. The shape of the country suddenly erased.

You don't know, he could have said, where you are. There literally is no country to know well or otherwise. Only bruising, relentless whiteness. Inside you, driving you, battering you. It pitches you here or there or nowhere when it finishes with you.

Instead of saying numerous things he could have said, he praises God for preserving him. Thanks her and the man Liam, *your husband, may I presume, madam*, for coming to his assistance.

Grateful beyond words, madam. God was truly with me. Delivered me to your generous hands. I feel His spirit in this house. In your charity toward a stranger. He's a merciful god, indeed.

Yes, she says. Yes yes yes. And those were his howling wolves at your heels last night, young man. If Liam hadn't dragged you in, they'd be gnawing your marrow bones this morning.

God granted me life. My life His to take away. My only desire is to serve Him. Preach His word. If He decides in His infinite wisdom that wild beasts should feed upon my flesh, so be it. A day is coming, soon enough, in God's good time, when wolf and lion and lamb shall lie down together.

Amen. And I hope it will be the lamb's day to eat the lion. Drink your tea while it's hot. Your flesh a block of ice when Liam laid you down.

My garments, good lady.

Wet. I've gathered them up and spread them near the fire. You wouldn't want to be wearing them now, I promise you, sir. Here. Take this and cover your shoulders. Luckily, you are young and strong. In a day or so you'll forget all of this, forget how near you were to death.

Beg pardon, madam. Not you good people who rescued me. I won't forget you.

You preach, then. An exhorter.

A humble servant of God. I serve Him in every way I am able.

A boy preacher.

God makes no distinction of person. He calls those He would call. All of us children in His sight.

A proud boy preacher.

Forgive me, madam. I did not intend to puff up my worthiness. I am indeed young and a novice in the Lord's service. My enthusiasm often outstrips my judgment. I beseech you. Do not mistake my eagerness for pride.

A pretty speech. Hush and drink your tea, boy preacher. You are quite agile in your apologies. They aren't needed here. I'm teasing you. Forgive an old woman's prying and silliness. Few strangers pass this way. I've lost the art of polite conversation. I'm drawing you out when I should allow you to rest, sir. Besides, I must be about my business.

Her long hair is drying to its actual colors. As many strands of gray and white as dull red. October grass. It must have been glorious before it was this, a thinning, faded cowl to her shoulders. Green eyes in a face lined by many sketches, ghost portraits vying with each other to present the truest image. Her green eyes rendered once. Original, abiding, sovereign in their dark-rimmed sockets. They silence bickering lines, reconcile quarreling versions of her likeness.

Thus began my stay with the Stubbses. In a region of scattered farms, their holding more inaccessible than most. As Mrs. Stubbs promised, few visitors appeared. No commonly traveled road led to their dwelling. Only someone determined to seek them out, or lost as I was the night of the storm, would worry their door. In effect a kind of hermitage. They'd sought, for various reasons, isolation, and isolation had embraced them, draped their lives it seemed in an obscurity almost total.

To escape the madness, Liam would exclaim. Once you've witnessed the madness, why would a sane man not run from it as fast and far as legs could carry him. The madness claims I'm not a man. Yet what the whites fear most is my power to do what only men can do. This old woman fetching our supper from the hearth, there was a day she'd stir a lust in any man. Flashing green eyes, milk-white skin. When she loosed it, a trophy of red hair down past her slender waist. The same fire she stirred in their loins stirring in mine and that was reason enough in their minds to murder me. Madness. Madness anyone not mad would flee.

*

She said it had frightened her at first. How much my presence changed Liam. More words spoken in an hour than she'd heard from him in a year. You thawed him, she told me, just as surely as we thawed you. I worried about a change in him so abrupt and complete, she said. A candle bristles, flares one last time before it dies, does it not. The man had turned himself into a desert of silence and then one day pails, showers, torrents of words. What would the effort cost him. Why all these stories now.

For more years than I care to count I've lived with a man whose silence has transformed him into a stranger. I made my peace. He was a familiar stranger. My stranger. I forgot whatever it was I once expected from life with a man. My history a sorry tale of surrendering, burying my hopes. My expectations came to matter less and less as I lived out the life that was mine, tied to a man who became impersonal and intimate as weather. I could not convince myself I was content, no, but contentment another country, and I resigned myself to residing here, in this separate place to which I've become accustomed.

Then you arrived. I lost one stranger, gained two. Liam began to talk again. Talk, talk, talking. Telling tales of England and Africa I'd forgotten, stories I'd never heard before. Master again of talk that had wooed me a lifetime ago. It was my ear he first seduced. How many days did I exhaust myself waiting for his trippingly light tread down the back staircase of the great house in Liverpool. Hungry for the feast of his voice, the little ditties he'd whistle or hum to himself.

I was a poor servant girl, possessed nothing but the curse of youthful beauty. Empty-headed, empty-handed, no family, only the certainty that men were my sole hope and protection, the certainty they would use me, hurt me, discard me. A pretty bauble for their pleasure. Grateful for the smallest kindnesses. Never expecting kindness. Believing myself unworthy. Surprised by kindness because many of these gentlemen dedicated themselves to teaching me my unworthiness. After pleasuring themselves upon me, they'd mark me with teeth, fists, feet, a riding crop. Tithes I must pay, as if I'd sought the men out, shamed them, as if I'd stolen something precious from them.

I would hear Liam on the stairs of the master's house and know he was bringing me a gift. As eager to talk to me as I was eager to listen. The gift of his words painting worlds for me. He'd voyaged round the globe, fought in great naval battles, escaped the chains and torture of a dungeon, lived among savages in faraway lands. Whether I was alone or the kitchen was filled with scullery maids preparing a banquet for the great folk upstairs, he let me know with his eyes and gestures, the inclination of his head, the tale he poured forth was meant especially for me.

Of course I fell in love. Of course his stories a baited hook.

We ran away. But what chance did we have, white woman, African man, for a life anywhere. Me bound to a long term of service, him bound forever by the darkness of his skin. Welcome nowhere except as servants.

We escaped across an ocean. Finally settled here, at the edge of the wilderness. Our flight exhausted us. Changed us. We became different people here. We lied in order to be accepted. Then began to live the lie. Like my memories of other, better times — of stories that undressed my heart, of stolen kisses, of dizzying waves of heat when our bodies secretly brushed in a crowd — Liam receded. He spoke less and less often. I believed he'd forgotten how. Or if he'd not lost altogether the art of speaking, had decided it was frivolous. Not worth his time and effort. That I was not worth the effort.

Then he begins chattering to you, a stranger. A flood of words in this dry, dry house where I have often lain awake long after he's snoring, wondering if he ever dreamed of those story days and if in the dream sang again to me. Lying in the dark beside him, hoping a single note might escape from his dream world into this one.

Now he's talking again. And you, whoever you are, listening. Two strangers in my house.

We were gulled from our African families, taken up by the English to be trained as holy men. Ten of us. They calculated no more than half would survive the rigors of the voyage, the first year of England's foul diseases and fouler weather, the intellectual demands of the training. Our hosts seemed astonished when, after a year of the worst abuse they could heap upon us, eight remained standing. Or stooping, as might be said of some of my dark brethren, whose will and spirits had been totally subdued by odious treatment. Of the five they expected to survive, they presumed at least one would be seized by homesickness, the Ebo melancholy they call it, and rendered unsuitable, so provision had been made to board and train only four of us. During that miserable seasoning year we were forced to lie two to a cot intended for one, four to a room not large enough for two, our rations halved as well as our allotment of blankets and clothing, in order not to discommode our hosts.

I cannot say I was unhappy to be selected one of four sent off to learn a trade. Not *sent off* exactly. Indentured. Transported. Owing a lifetime of service to merchants who purchased us from the church.

Beg pardon. Not *purchased* exactly. A matter of our repaying to the church the expenses incurred in transporting us from Africa.

If given the choice to stay or leave the priest school, I most certainly would have chosen not to stay. I hated my life there. But rumors about the world outside our holy prison did not cause me to rejoice at being expelled. I was spared, of course, the onerous duty of choosing. Just as I had been spared the choice of leaving or staying in Mother Africa's bosom.

One ironical circumstance is, had I not been stolen from Africa, I would have become a holy man, a healer of soul and body in my homeland. My father was a renowned wizard. I would have been raised to succeed him. Molded to be worthy of assuming his mantle. My formal initiation had not begun. I recall only a great spotted cape, fear and respect of my father's powers. How he could change his shape or disappear instantly. How he could be many different places at once.

A Mr. Stubbs compensated the church for its expenditures upon me, gained in turn the right to work me to death. Eventually I became manservant and companion to Stubbs' son, George. I learned much from this George Stubbs. Under his influence I began to draw pictures, think of myself as an artist of sorts. Which suggests that sometime during this period of my life I rebuilt considerable self-respect and confidence in my abilities. Remade myself, I believe it's fair to say.

Liam fits two halves of a cracked plate together.

Ha. You see. Almost as good as new. I wish I'd held up as well over the years. One clean break down the middle. Not a terrible price to pay for survival, is it.

I have none of his drawings. But George Stubbs was an artist. A very considerable artist, I assure you. I saved this plate. It traveled with us on the ship from England because the plate reminds me of my life there. The good and the bad.

No. Though we favor one another superficially, I am not the model from whose likeness the Negro on the plate is taken. In the taverns of London today I have no doubt you'd meet many who'd claim to be the emblem's original.

George Stubbs gave me the plate. Presented it along with a brief speech about freedom, man's dignity and evil, a mumbled preamble we both suffered through politely. He had received the plate from the very hand of its maker, the famous Mr. Josiah Wedgwood himself. Just about the time Stubbs released me from his service, he was commissioned to execute portraits of Josiah Wedgwood and family. Wedgwood would have had his pick of artists. His patronage of George Stubbs attests to Stubbs' stature and skill.

This is the commemorative plate designed and manufactured by Wedgwood as a weapon in the anti-slavery campaign. Notice how the kneeling Negro in chains at the center of it is ringed by the motto *Am I not a man and a brother*. Looking at the design now, I see the circle of words as another chain.

The good and bad. Stubbs one of my benefactors. And, indeed, a friend. Because of the circumstances under which I received the gift of this plate, Stubbs, not the Negro, is the centerpiece. I see a sooty Stubbs crouched there, eternally pleading his cause. Asking me, once his property, to acknowledge his membership in the brotherhood of man.

Your god, preacher. You profess to love him. How can you love a cruel god.

Beg pardon, good lady. He is a most kind and merciful master.

Kindness his worst cruelty. In his world one beast must devour another to survive. I understand such a law, such a world. Whether it pleases me or not, there is sense in it. It plays no favorites. One law — eat or be eaten — rules. All creatures must obey it. But then your god introduces the lie of kindness. Tempts men to believe there is another path, a way to cheat this iron-clad rule.

He whispers poison in your ear. Tells you that you are different, better than other creatures. An exception atop some airy pedestal. He whispers you are his favorite, exempt from the law governing all living things.

He beguiles you with the false promise of a different world, different rules. Confuses you, plagues you. You question yourself, torture yourself. You forget the nature of the actual world you inhabit. You yearn for an impossible one ruled by kindness. God's kindness that would mark you and others like you as special.

God tricks you. Teases you. Stuns you with unexpected kindnesses. A bounteous harvest. A sunset. Mother's love. Rare tastes now and then of kindness. Promises always of more.

To what end. You should know and he surely knows the truth. The law. The circle out of which no creature is permitted to break. No exceptions. No favorites. Just some he fattens before the kill. Some he toys with.

You are too hard, madam.

Many who have deserted God rail at his unkindness toward humankind. Point at innocent babes slaughtered in their sleep. I can't forgive his kindness. No place for kindness in the world he's fashioned. Kindness an afterthought. Or premeditated mischief.

You would prefer a world stripped of kindness, Mrs. Stubbs. A world without hope or faith. Our eyes permanently fixed on the ground as we drag through the world expecting the worst.

Are you implying I'm ungrateful.

No, madam. I think you are unfair. Like a greedy merchant, you hide your hand below the scale and you tilt it. In this vale of tears certainly one should not blame God for sprinkling kindness and mercy upon our poor bowed heads.

God is not the sinner, good lady. In spite of our great fall, our undeservingness, we are suffered here on earth to receive a fore-taste of a better world that awaits us. Surely you would not pray that these simple joys be withheld.

Are you offering me what your god never has offered. Are you granting me the kindness of a choice.

Choice.

Yes. The choice of being something other than a puppet, a slave, eternally in God's debt. I refuse the terms of his bargain. I choose to trade at a different stall altogether. None of your sin and guilt, life everlasting and everlasting damnation. I don't want a god with answers, nor one I must answer to. No god with a face, hands, words, feet. No features that remind me of myself nor of anyone else.

There is great anger in your voice. Have I offended. Beg pardon if I have, madam.

No one ever asked me. I was never given a choice. You think you've made a choice. In the end the choice you believe you've made, and mine, which I know to be no choice at all, are the same. Bring us to the same place. This place.

I'm afraid I don't understand you.

Yes. Nor I you. A kindness, no doubt. A kindness.

*

When he's working, the old man is tireless. Chopping firewood, digging a trench, sawing, plowing, planting, sowing, his lean body repeats the monotonous motions unflaggingly, doggedly, at a rate not fast but steady, steady, requiring all my strength to match. No overseer with whip, curses and threats could have driven me as hard. Only the old man's example, his tenacity and total concentration, keeps me laboring alongside him to match his pace. His age more than double, perhaps more than triple mine. A man of my middling height but thinnish. At first glance I mistook him for a scrawny fellow. Since he almost never removed his shirt, a brown, long-sleeved, sweat-stained affair, as crusty and indestructible as its owner, I didn't see his bare back and arms until one afternoon she sat him on a stump in the yard and rubbed a pungent salve of roots and herbs she had concocted into his skin. A body of dark cords, braided, twisted, knotted, shining as her hands anointed it.

He claimed he'd once carried a horse on his shoulders up a flight of stairs. In England, working for George Stubbs. Said others credited Stubbs with this feat, but no, no. George Stubbs carried the stripped carcass down the stairs after having his way with it. The horse much lighter then.

My master a strong enough man. Stronger than most. George Stubbs had offered to assist me in packing the beast up the steps, but the stairwell too narrow and turned too sharply. No room for a dead horse and two live men.

Once I was under the horse, once my knees braced beneath it, a matter of balance. Getting under it, balancing the weight rather than hefting it.

My sole concern that the ancient stairs of Stubbs' cottage might not bear the burden of man and beast simultaneously. Fortunately, they held. No doubt the fact I've never been a heavy man, always a man light on my feet, contributed mightily to the stairs' forbearance.

After I had toted the horse upstairs and we had it hanging from the rafters, Stubbs was delighted. Thrust a half-crown in my hand. Called me for weeks afterward Centaur. His ebony Centaur.

When Liam stops working, you'd think he'll never begin again. He sinks. Ashen and drawn. Utterly still. Too much, you think. The old fellow has essayed too much this time. Nothing left. His eyes closed. Sweat glistening on his bald head, in runnels filling the creases of his face, pooling in his beard, bleeding through the shirt. He slouches further into himself. Is he shrinking. Is he trying to hide or has the feverish effort melted him. If he sits motionless for an hour, all his substance will drain into the soil. I'll run to the house and fetch her. Bring her to the spot. I'm sorry. So sorry. Nothing's left. Just the dark, damp circle you see there.

You think nothing on earth will raise him from his stupor. Then he begins talking. I'm sprawled nearby, feeling nearly as tired as he looks. He knows I'm there. Knows I'm listening, never stop listening.

Abruptly, as a story stops, we're on our feet again. Heating up again to achieve the precise tempo when you are the work and the work is you. No separation. Nothing but work. Its rhythm inside you, what you are.

I was panyared from my country and brought to England to learn the business of tending the immortal souls of men. Instead, a year after my arrival, I found myself in a butcher shop, indentured to the trade of slaughtering and skinning animals, curing their hides.

Overnight I was transported from the oppressive silence and isolation of the seminary where they had interned us — a pitiful coffle of African boys who were to be whipped, starved, bullied and buggered into becoming holy men — transported from there to the hulking sheds and brutal pens of the tannery owned by Stubbs Senior, the father of George Stubbs.

After my year in the rural seminary, the teeming port of Liverpool would have been shock enough. Imagine, then, my confusion when in addition to the city's assault on my senses, the stench and tumult of a tannery exploded in my face. We'd heard tales before we were kidnaped from our African homes of cannibals who lived across the great water. The first day in the tannery, overwhelmed by clamor, stink, rivers of blood, I feared I had stumbled into the very establishment where the pink eaters of men prepared their unnatural feasts.

I listen to Liam and try to imagine the frightening scene as it unfolds before the eyes of an African boy, a boy a few years younger than myself, a boy in that strange English country, a country unknown to him and unknown to me, and the boy's home another country even further away, a country he would know as I know this Pennsylvania through which I am riding, blue sky overhead, bouncing with Liam on the seat of a wagon loaded with lumber we've chopped and sawed from forests as familiar to me as the vast forests of another land across the sea are to the boy who enters the slaughterhouse, hears the moaning and braying, the panicked squeals of captive animals who smell blood, hear on every side the death wails of their tribes. He sees fresh carcasses hoisted on hooks to the ceiling timbers, entrails spilling to form steaming puddles on the sawdusted floor. One of his duties will be to scrape this foul, slippery ooze out the door he is entering now, sweep it into open gutters that run by the sheds, where gory ditches of offal thicken and putrefy.

Cries of animals dying, men shouting, cursing, grunting as they deliver blows with mallet, cleaver and ax, men thrusting deep, slicing deep with sharp blades that sometimes strike bone and splinter, inflicting wounds on those who wield them. Beast blood, man blood, mingled on the knives, noises of men and beasts mixed indistinguishably in the din assaulting the boy's ears.

I learn quickly. Whether it's how to shepherd souls to heavenly pastures or how to chop and skin the bodies of those miserable animals in the charnel house. In twelve months I'd mastered reading, writing and sums tolerably well, had committed innumerable passages of scripture to memory, though I often had no notion of the meaning of the orphaned words I parroted for my tutors. In far less time I learned how to transform live beasts to hides, the bloody, magical process by which the elder Stubbs earned his living as a currier. A rudimentary understanding of the process, to be sure, but a far more comprehensive knowledge than that of any of my colleagues, who seemed content to master one task of the many required to manufacture leather.

My diligence, dependability and tirelessness were noticed. They earned me rapid advancement, that is to say, more duties, and of course more beatings. My fellow workers, a passive, besotted, surly lot, didn't like to see a black boy slip past them, even though they exercised neither intelligence nor effort to advance themselves. The only task they accomplished with vigor: drubbings they administered to the cheeky African boy. Nevertheless, I was in demand, gained the grudging confidence of my superiors because I labored four times as hard as my rough peers. Though I was valued not half as much as the others, my worth to the company was double that of any white man.

Peculiar arithmetic, isn't it. You'd do well to learn the lesson in it. You shall observe the same peculiar arithmetic applied to the accounting today when we sell these logs.

When first we arrived in this neighborhood some twenty years ago, we depended upon a dead man for protection. The name I gave the dead man was Stubbs. She was Mrs. Stubbs. I chose the name because I knew George Stubbs would have enjoyed the ruse. He'd teased me often with ironical names. Baptized me Centaur. Othello. Hannibal. Aesop. Called my face his map of Africa. Stealing Stubbs' name a trick to protect ourselves. White woman and black man setting up in a household together as precarious in this country then as it remains today. So she advertised herself as Mrs. Stubbs, an English gentlewoman, relic of Mr. George Stubbs, traveling with her husband's trusted slave, Liam.

She was uncommonly handsome in her widow's weeds. Created a small stir when she arrived in this neighborhood, but let it be known immediately to the local squires who presented themselves her determination to live alone.

We ensconced ourselves far from curious, prying eyes. The widow bereft, inconsolable, sworn never to marry again, faithful to her husband till she reunites with him in the grave. The equally faithful slave humble and close-mouthed when he appears in public, which I seldom did, to purchase provisions or trade the produce of the grieving widow's farm.

It's in Mrs. Stubbs' name, as her servants, that we sell this timber. The price we will receive is double at least what would be paid to two free men of color. England, these United States, the Indies — wherever they enslave us, the odd arithmetic bleeds us.

When by halves the worth of our labor is steadily diminished till it is of no value at all to us, then we who claim to be free are rendered as powerless as our brethren in chains. I call the whites' attitudes toward us madness. But if truth be told, there is policy in the madness. Policy. Evil, cunning arithmetic.

Though I was still *boy* and *nigger* to the rawest, lowest laborer in the tannery and subject still to the most brutal tasks of hacking and hauling if ordered to them, as messenger and jack-of-all-trades I became the elder Stubbs' eyes and ears, his sable Mercury. My miscellaneous duties conferred an immunity of sorts. Kept me running from one end of the establishment to another, from the animal pens reeking of dung and fear to the wainscoted offices where clerks in silk coats whispered and tiptoed so as not to disturb the tyrant's sleep, his sessions with starving country girls and prostitutes his agents culled from Liverpool's dockside alleys.

Because he understood my worth, my loyalty secured by his absolute power over my fate, the elder Stubbs furloughed me to serve and spy upon his son. The son's lack of interest in the tannery did not please the father and occasioned much ill will between them. However, they shared an inordinate obstinacy, mutually acknowledged and respected. Young Stubbs had determined to be an artist, an artist of an unusual kind, since what he wished to draw and paint was stamped indelibly by his early years in his father's house, his father's factory.

After an unsatisfactory apprenticeship to a local portrait painter, the younger Stubbs moved to York and set up shop on his own, swearing never again to learn nature through the eyes of another painter but to work only from the source itself. He would observe and copy nature directly. Study nature by lifting her gown and peering underneath.

His special pursuit, not surprisingly, was the science of anatomy. His father confided to me once in a tone mixing pride with distaste how at six years old his boy had cut open a cat, at eight a puppy, producing very pretty sketches of the innards of both creatures. Not only would Stubbs lift nature's petticoat and stare, he would flay her layer by layer, pursue her mysteries down to the bone. Further if he could.

This project caused him to fall in with a disreputable lot of medical men who shared his unwholesome interest in the dissection of cadavers. Included in this set were man-midwives, as they were satirically known in York, with their curious surgical instruments and more curious fascination with the private parts of ladies.

Though from a distance, in the son's obsession with cutting and skinning, one could detect a kind of backhanded homage to his father's trade, the house where he'd been raised with death as neighbor, squealing cattle, sheep bleating their death moans just beyond the door of his nursery, the father was not pleased. Especially since not only decent citizens but the law frowned upon the gruesome practice of human dissection. Caught tampering with a corpse, a man could be fined heavily or imprisoned, to say nothing of the vile reputation that attached itself to anyone in any manner suspected of such blasphemous trespass.

But fascination with the science of anatomy, the practice of dissection as a means to unlock the secrets of the human body, continued to rage unabated in York and other English cities. Medical doctors, the odd enthusiast or artist like Stubbs, would go to any lengths to procure specimens for their researches. Trade in cadavers was illegal, thus highly profitable. An underground commerce thrived. The body snatchers who trafficked in corpses were known as resurrectionists, and a ruthless, depraved crew they were. Depending on such rogues to supply their needs placed honest, well-intentioned gentlemen in jeopardy.

Stubbs Senior presented me as a birthday gift to his son. He extolled my virtues as a manservant, though I'd never in my life performed one minute in that capacity for any soul on earth. He enjoined me privately to certain duties, which if I defaulted, he promised, would most certainly bring dire consequences upon my then woolly head. He expected me to protect his son from the villainous grave robbers, avoid embarrassing entanglements with the law and finally report to him regularly on his son's activities.

As you might well imagine, my duties ran me ragged. A saving grace in my situation was young Stubbs' habit of treating me more as companion than servant in his adventures and misadventures. We roamed York's streets together, welcome in the comfortable chambers of the prosperous medical fraternity, greeted with ribald toasts in the low taverns where unsavory business with the resurrectionists was transacted.

During this period in York I accompanied Stubbs to many a lying-in. I assisted, you might say, at the debut of various souls who may be walking the streets of York today.

Sir John Burton was a particular friend and patron of young Stubbs. Sir John had engaged him to illustrate a manual on midwifery he, Burton, had penned. Impressed by Stubbs' growing expertise, he would also send him private students for lessons in the science of anatomy. In a sense these two gentlemen shared corpses, and thus forged a unique partnership. They became thick as thieves. Which in actuality they were, since they depended on resurrectionists to supply the cadavers necessary to their mutual enterprises. Intrigue, danger, the excitement of exploring uncharted territory, charged the air of those York years.

One rainy evening in late spring we went in a coach with Burton and Smellie, another intrepid physician determined to out-midwife the midwives of York. We were received at an elegant home in a fashionable quarter. Entering through the tradesmen's door at the rear of a courtyard, we were bustled downstairs unceremoniously into a dim chamber off the kitchen, where we donned women's smocks and aprons, then lappeted bonnets to crown our ensembles. The hilarity of the coach, encouraged by a bottle of Madeira consumed to raise our spirits and prepare us for the humiliating conditions that were part of the bargain Burton and Smellie had struck to gain permission to conduct the lying-in, lapsed, after the silliness of gowning ourselves, to a lugubrious solemnity. As if we'd been called not to a birth but a funeral.

Single file, we trooped back up the stairs, retaining as much dignity as possible in our smocks, aprons and caps. No vow of silence bound us, yet not a word leaked as we followed a maid to her lady's bedroom. Silence violated only by Burton's cough, the telltale bag of instruments in Smellie's hand, clanging as we negotiated a twist in the narrow, unlit stairwell.

The lady herself, supported by a sea of brightly colored and patterned satin pillows, reclined against the padded headboard of her bed. Four braces of candles illuminated the scene, one at each corner of the canopied bed. Beside each candelabrum a female servant stood stiffly at attention.

The patient was draped in layers of rich fabric. An indigo turban billowed about her head. I glimpsed fear, surprise, shyness felt or artfully mimed before she hid her eyes.

Sir John bowed, or should I say curtsied, to his hostess, since the rules of our female masquerade seemed to extend to all particulars. A dumb show it was to be, since the gruff, coarse grunt of male voices, we'd been warned, would offend the lady's modesty as much as men's eyes or hands.

A batting of her false eyelashes, a further demure drop of chin to ample bosom, was all the acknowledgment Sir John received for his bow/curtsy, or curtsy/bow, and it seemed to suit him just fine, because he nodded to his colleague and they commenced.

I wondered how much of the mound on the bed, puffed up like some preposterous meringue, was blanket, how much was belly. A bizarre tale circulating in the coffeehouses concerned a young giant-bellied woman, Mary Tolf of Godalming, who, as the tale would have it, littered rabbits, two dozen of them alive and dead. I saw Burton pulling strings of children, plump, identical little sausages, an endless chain of paper dolls, from the cornucopia beneath the candy-striped quilt.

How did the surgeons intend to extricate the lady from her soft armor without violating her modesty. As the good doctors approached the bed, I half expected the female servants to form an Amazonian phalanx to block the men's path. Certainly the experiment must terminate here, now. How could the lady be both decorous and naked. Two deliveries, not one. Madam must be coaxed from the bedclothes before the infant could be extracted from her womb. The first delivery a matter of far more delicacy and diplomatic maneuvering than the second.

Though neither was a large man, Burton and Smellie were good-sized women, one short and thick, the other tallish but slight. Their voluminous smocks cast bulky shadows flitting on the walls and ceiling as they moved — nay, swished — to the foot of the bed. The female attendants seemed to have rehearsed their roles and assisted the doctors in disposing of excess pillows, removing blankets and sheets, folding others up toward the head of the bed. From where I stood with Stubbs a hillock of linens obscured the gentlewoman's face. Stubbs stepped closer and I followed, anticipating no role myself except to indulge my curiosity and protect my charge from harm.

A sort of cavern or tunnel had formed in the hill of bedclothes, its highest elevation the thrust of the lady's stomach. The tunnel's walls sloped symmetrically to either side of the bed. A cave that candlelight barely penetrated, its recesses totally hidden when the doctors' shadows fell across the entrance.

Closer, the overpowering scent of perfume wafts from beneath the bedding. A French essence, no doubt, to disguise the raw Anglo-Saxon odors of birth.

Smellie shooed the women away from the foot of the bed. The eldest of the attendants reached down and touched her mistress's hand, smiled at her with tight-lipped compassion. The others returned to their original posts, eyes fixed on the middle distance, blind witnesses seeing no evil, their incontestable respectability receiving no taint from the unusual proceedings, these costumed men usurping women's places.

Velvet slippers on the lady's feet, soft purple bootees with a gold braided drawstring at the ankles. For the first time I thought of her as something other than a receptacle containing a package we'd come to liberate. Her ankles slim, well turned. A loose knot secured each slipper. In other circumstances I'd enjoy slowly unknotting the gold string. I'd play, rub my cheek against the furry pile, pinch the cord in thumb and finger, tease the tassels dangling from its ends.

The pace of the undertaking had slowed. The two physicians in their bonnets and gowns were studying one another now, as if they'd lost their way, as if they did not recognize each other in the ridiculous garb. In the cave mouth I could see hems of at least two garments just above the tops of the velvet slippers. Except to frown, the lady had not stirred since the little mute ceremony attending our entrance into the bedroom. Her back remained propped by pillows resting against the headboard, her limbs out-stretched flat on the bed, ankles not quite crossed but touching. Unless she planned to spit out the baby, and that was unlikely given the grim set of her mouth, no path for the infant's arrival lay open.

Then she groaned. A piteous, helpless, wincing groan ratchet-ing from belly to chest to throat, scraping something of her insides away with each fluctuation as the groan clawed its way out of her body. Three times she gasps, each gaining in intensity, a wave mounting another wave's back, doubling, tripling force as it runs against the shore.

Oh Mary, Mother of God. Oh. Ohh. Ohhhh.

A second maid grasps the lady's free hand. The matronly wom-an leans over the sufferer, whispering, encouraging, cooing. Their shadows engulf the head of the bed, dash about the room, pan-icked wings fluttering.

There is a thrashing. An audible clicking of teeth. A spasm draws up the lady's limbs. Gown, shift, chemise, fall away, pooling under her naked hips. Burton's sure hands on her steepled knees, guiding them, slowing the whiplashing to a gentle rock back and forth, back and forth. As he calms her, he slowly eases her bare legs apart.

Simple after that. Pain. Then a laying on of hands. Cure.

Simple, but long, messy and loud. I was sure Stubbs recognized as I did the noises of the slaughterhouse. Blood gushing, blood painting flesh. Grunts and pants and squeals at this end of the business too. She could not have seen Smellie undo the rattling sack of instruments, yet she must have heard it and understood the coldness, the cruel shapes of hook and plier and rod and spatula and bulbous-headed cylinder. Smellie opened the bag during a quiet pause in her labor, and I know she must have heard it, because she loosed the most abandoned and affrighted of her screeches.

Throughout, I noticed Stubbs' eyes casting about the room. What was he searching for. Was the spectacle of new life emerging less interesting in its volatile squirminess than something he might spy dead in a corner or pinned to the wall, a specimen that would not move while his patient, meticulous gaze, his sharp knives, penetrated its secrets.

Or was Stubbs embarrassed. An unclothed body natural to him, but partial nudity, the revealing gowns of ladies in their sitting rooms, the coquettish exposing of breast or thigh by tavern bawds, paintings with fig leaves, statues decorously draped, offended him. He emanated prudishness odd in one who professed no religion nor conventional morality apart from respect and admiration for nature's disciplined order as it evinced itself in all things alive and once alive. Perhaps it was the naked legs. Those same pale legs, flayed of skin, peeled to reveal sinew and tendon, would have usurped Stubbs' undivided attention. But separated from the trunk of the woman's body, alive and kicking, the legs to him might very well have been obscene. Dead, drawn and quartered another matter altogether.

The lady's name escapes me now. Tis no matter, since she

died soon after. Of the child, the purple slippers, no further intelligence came our way.

On another occasion, after protracted secret negotiations between
Burton and an Italian gentleman who professed a passionate interest in Burton's endeavor to replace old superstitions and dangerous traditions adhering to midwifery with practice based on science and reason, Stubbs and I were invited again to view a birth.

The same rigmarole — coach sent for us at night, female ap-
parel, creeping through servants' entrances, etc. No female attendants this time, only a patient in a drab room, supine on a bed,
blanket drawn to chin, a bump in the middle of the blanket as if a
pillow had been stuffed under it.

And not the plain, homespun, smockish costumes of our previous outing. Fancy gowns this time, too small to squeeze into
without undressing. Frilly gowns, beribboned, brightly colored,
pleated, flounced. In spite of the usual ration of wine, Smellie had
balked.

Burton. I can't continue in this manner. I am not a monkey.
Nor a clown. I am a serious man of science, here to protect some
silly creature's life, the life of her offspring. And look at me. Regard
yourself, sir. And them. My god, the lot of us, a troupe escaped
from Bedlam. Why not our own garments, at the very least.

Our host insisted we must submit to his wife's demands and be
appareled in clothes familiar to her.

A pox on them both.

Come, come now. Clothes do not make the man.

No. They make us women. Damned foolish women. Sneaking
about in the dark. Afraid of our shadows.

Shhh, Smellie. We have entered willingly into this bargain.

We've weighed the costs, and these costumes a small price to pay after all.

It's enough that we must sort through the endless rags in which the women hide themselves. Like unwrapping an Egyptian mummy.

Mummy. Mummy indeed. You are in good form tonight, Smellie.

Mind your tongue, Stubbs.

Beg pardon, madam.

Dammit, man.

Shhhh. Let's get on with it. We'll talk later. Over another bottle. Many bottles, if you please, of my best Madeira, Smellie. Come on, good fellow.

Again the bowing curtsy. The agreed-upon silence once we're in milady's presence.

The chamber brightly lit. Small, undistinguished, cramped by a bed and two tables. A curtain ceiling to floor immediately behind the bed. One table drawn up bedside, upon which Smellie deposited the instruments. The inevitable metallic clunk. Basins of water and clean lengths of cloth on the other table. All in order.

Below the turban, which seemed the fashion then for lyings-in, an ugly patient appeared barely awake. I prepared myself for screams. The jig of pain. I was a veteran. Ready this time for the transmogrifying agonies of labor. I huddled with Stubbs as far away from the bed as the room allowed. Once labor began in earnest we would tip closer. The patient, absorbed by the throbbing whirl of pain between her legs, would neither notice nor care.

Smellie lifted the bottom edge of the sheet. I recalled velvet slippers, a comely ankle. His arm snaked under the cover. Then the covering was a snake swallowing his arm by inches. Then a serpent sure enough struck.

Smellie's hand still clutched one hairy ankle as the man's other leg kicked back the sheet.

Ho. What's this.

Foul play. Foul play.

The room was instantly full. A company of men had burst from behind the arras. Shouting, laughing, slapping each other's backs, twisting themselves into grotesque parodies of extravagant merriment. Coughing, spitting their glee. Tongues clucking, fingers wagging. A fat fellow so overcome he's down on one knee.

A great joke. The company gloriously pleased with themselves. All with bottles and glasses in hand. One brays like a donkey, another mimics Smellie's high voice. *What's this. What's this*, his fist clutching his scrotum, shaking an imaginary member as the hairy, naked lout on the bed had wiggled his enormous tool in response to the good doctor's question.

What's this. What's this.

Aren't they positively gorgeous. Such beauties. Hear, hear. What lovely nymphs and naiads. Ahhh. What have we here. One of Ethiop's daughters. Look at that one's fat bum. Naughty, naughty lasses, and so on and so on, an endless barrage of such drollery and worse skewered and scorched the men-midwives.

Fortunately, it had been a scheme to humiliate and nothing more. It could have been worse, far worse. The elaborate hoax, though mean-spirited, was not meant to injure the victims or alert the authorities. Many whom Burton and Smellie considered friends and colleagues were among the perpetrators. Rather than join the mob, however, the good doctors departed in a huff.

Stubbs and I, being thicker-skinned and, besides, not the exact targets of the prank, remained women through the night, drinking and carousing till the cock crowed.

When I married her off to Stubbs, I purloined his name also. She was Mrs. George Stubbs. As family retainer and property, in a sense I too bore the Stubbs name. A darker brother. I could see Stubbs shaking his grizzled head. Choosing a wife for him, killing him off before he could enjoy his prize, claiming his name and wife for myself. Had I carried the game too far. Would Stubbs be amused.

I enjoyed no success fixing Stubbs' character for her. She'd shrug in disbelief when I described his habits. The more circumstantial my recounting, the less she seemed able to construct a whole, believable personage from the details I elaborated. His exceedingly long walks through the countryside around Horkstow, his abstemiousness once he'd settled away from York. No strong drink. Little food and of the plainest sort, with little or no variety in his meals. His helpmate, Mrs. Morgan, always at his beck and call, his shadow when he allowed her to assist in his strange enterprises. They spoke to one another without speaking. I was not familiar with this woman's history, nor with how she and Stubbs had become attached. During their courtship I'd been back in the tannery, serving out my eternal term. I hadn't glimpsed George Stubbs for years when, upon his father's death, I was summoned again to serve the son.

I don't know why exactly I felt compelled to describe for my lady Stubbs' quirks and tics. I also praised his consummate skill at drawing, his tireless dedication to any task he'd set for himself. Was he proof before my eyes that to be an artist was to be afflicted with an irresistible obsession. The power of Stubbs' obsession lent it a sort of purity. As light bent through a prism displays itself in all its rainbowed glory, Stubbs' dedication to dissecting and drawing revealed aspects of his character otherwise unknown, unseen. Watching him draft adroitly, with endless patience, his studies of skeletons, of exposed musculature, the intricate webbing of veins that circulate the blood, of organs removed from the body's deepest cavities, I observed the hidden colors in Stubbs, how they made themselves known only through his creations. I envied him. Wished for a task, an art, that might focus my powers in the manner Stubbs directed his.

I think now that I was using Stubbs to tell her my story. My feelings about him were vexed. I admired what made him an artist. I also recoiled because his obsession led to a monkish existence, unnatural detachment from other human beings. He made me aware of a double lack in myself. A double hunger.

No story could explain my dissatisfaction with myself. Something crucial was missing. I couldn't name it, but serving and observing Stubbs, I began to recognize that his life, odd as it was, had substance, and mine was merely a shadow. Could it be because I possessed neither an art nor the ruthlessness necessary to acquire and practice one.

Stubbs' drawings, in spite of what they rendered, were beautiful. But if they'd been ugly, I still would have envied whatever it was inside him driving him to do them. The light passing through him into his pictures was a light I desperately wished to uncover in myself. I envied his independence, his decision to seize life, do with it as he saw fit. Envied his freedom to be obsessed.

I wanted to know his secret. How could he treat his life as he treated those carcasses we'd push an iron rod through, then fasten hooks to the rod, hoist the specimen with tackle and pulley so he could flay and fillet and scoop it out, recording at every stage what his unblinking eye perceived. As much a record of disappearances as a portrait of what was present, the tangible blood and flesh and bone hanging there, perpetually giving way to what was next and next and next.

Stubbs had no life to speak of, once he dedicated himself wholly to his art. Or myriad lives, each so transient he could dismiss them, dispatch them, paying little or no attention to the conventions governing the lives of others. Stubbs a fine instrument — a metal pen, a sable brush — and his life a sheath where the instrument was stored. All his effort was freeing himself to perform the task for which the instrument had been honed. Any sort of life or none suitable, as long as the instrument was protected, as long as it could be efficiently disengaged and employed.

Stubbs had taught me to be unsatisfied. Taught me what I lacked. My stories about Stubbs were not simply reminiscences. I was trying to warn her. About the future, our prospects for a life together in this New World. Crossing the ocean, I expected the colors inside me would be freed. I knew I couldn't tolerate anything less than what Stubbs granted himself. Not one life, black man and white woman in a cage others fashioned, but what was next and next and next.

For a while after we settled here I tried to find the light. It wasn't to be. I grew more and more silent. My vocation became merely to watch the light inside myself dim, flicker, expire. A duty I devoted myself to so fiercely it became my art, a terrible denying of the light.

This New World a graveyard for African people. We were brought here to serve and die. Serve or die.

Stubbs drew pictures of what people ordinarily couldn't see. His studies of dissected cadavers exposed a bloody universe beneath the skin. Bloody but ordered. Once revealed, it couldn't be denied. He'd copied nature, the truth inside us all. What art could I invent to expose the lie of the madness. What specimens could I hang up and flay. How many layers peel from a white body to free the black, how many from a black body to release the white.

Of course I didn't learn what I'm telling you in the time it takes to tell. I'm just beginning to understand after years of silence why I lost the urge to paint, to speak. Why I lived as I did. How the madness crushes the best in us.

What attracted me to Stubbs, what made me unhappy with myself, doubt myself, could not be resolved in a country where madness reigns. The madness driving men to trade in human flesh, buying and selling one another like wood, or cattle. How could I be an artist in a land prospering from such commerce. We fled from England but found nothing different here. More space, perhaps, more places to hide, but the same air thick with blood and wailing. We were forced to lie when we arrived on these shores. Forced to quarantine ourselves.

Here I began to see that the seeds of the madness were also the seeds of Stubbs' art. His obsession part of what nourished the madness.

In London Stubbs had pointed out a toy in an oculist's shop. A cylinder ingeniously fitted with mirrors and stained glass inside. You peer through the eyepiece, twist the tube and see colorful, intricate, everchanging designs. I often think of viewing Stubbs in such an instrument. Consider him, his license and single-mindedness, his selfishness and self-absorption. Now twist slightly, the image becomes Stubbs Senior, his tannery, an empire built corpse by corpse. Given another small turn, the commerce in beasts becomes commerce in men.

I would not want a world bereft of Stubbs' pictures. But the price. The terrible, mad price. What was the man seeking. How much was he willing to destroy to find it. How much of what is natural in man was he willing or driven to set aside as he pursued whatever he was pursuing. Stripping layer after layer from dead animals.

Dismissing my life, my connections with other lives, didn't earn me a new life here. I couldn't fall in love with death, but I let love die. Lost my woman. Would pretty pictures have eased the pain.

He pours water nearly scalding slowly into one end of the tub he'd fashioned from a barrel. She shivers as its fire spreads through the pool to her ankles. She crouches. Slowly squats.

Hot. Hot.

Too hot.

No, just right. Thank you. I'm fine now. Leave me now.

Her eyes snap up at him. She'd been listening to him talk about Stubbs a long time without responding.

How could Stubbs sit day after day closed up in a room with his nose inches away from the moldering corpse of a horse. How could the woman abide the stench in her house. How did you assist him without gagging. Why didn't you cut down the putrefying beast.

Wonderful drawings, you say. Nature revealed, you say. The science of anatomy advanced. To what end.

Where are the drawings. Who sees them. These doctors who have unmasked nature's secrets, do they treat you or me. And if they arrived on the doorstep today, with all their science, could they make our lives better. Could they restore what's been torn apart.

I pretended not to hear her questions. Blamed her for missing the point. It's taken all these years to address what she asked. Only now, as my voice returns, speaking with you, am I ready to take up the conversation I fled.

Rain had not stopped them. But they stopped to watch it rain. Just inside the barn door he sprawls against a bundle of hay, legs stretched out before him, muddy feet some swamp predator's gory paws. Liam beside him, folded in half almost, resting on his haunches in that African squat he could hold motionless till the end of time.

Rain had begun the day before, lasted through the night. A gentle, saturating May rain, the first of the new month, rain that greened the land, the special long spring rain coming every year and transforming the woods overnight into a sea of green. You could see green in the rain. A bright sheen imparted to all growing things. Struck blind, he believed he'd hear green running in every leaf and blade of grass.

At dawn the sky brightened. Patches of whitish mist cocooned low-lying ground. Diamonds winked in the grass. Glistening tears of rain budded branches, bushes. A false clearing before clouds darkened and rain began again. Less a feel of rain falling while they worked than a sense the air was sweating, a soaking, pungent sweat turning them green as they hacked and dug at the earth.

He shivered. Once he stopped moving, his damp shirt was

heavy against his skin. Though the drizzling rain had seemed warm as pee, it chilled him now. About three hours since sunrise and the temperature rising steadily. He felt that too. As soon as they started working again, he'd miss the chill's bite, the shivering waves passing through his body like the caress of icy fingers.

What do you think, old man. Will it stop today.

By noon. Falling up now and crosswise as much as falling down. Hardly deserves the name of rain now. A scorching sun all afternoon, I wager. Bit of baking after the batter is moist and mixed.

If I were a betting man, I wouldn't wager against your wager. You know this land too well.

Know it. I don't claim to know it. I've become accustomed. That's all. My livelihood, as yours, reverend sir, requires a certain familiarity with the land's nasty habits. More to knowing it than simply having lived here long enough to recognize some of its tricks.

When I'm moldering in my grave, when I'm mud like those clods stuck to your boots, I won't know this land. I don't expect to rest in peace here even then. My dead bones no more welcome here than my live ones.

But you've stayed on. You've built this prosperous farm.

Yes. I'm old. And stuck. I'll die here. But I don't know this land. We've lain together in the same bed twenty years but I do not know it. Look around. Life everywhere. Fertile soil. Blooming life. You can smell the richness this morning. Hear the land drinking like a thirsty animal. Anything might grow here. Anything but my seed. I know my African seed shrivels here. Grows stunted and twisted if it grows at all. Tribes from all over the globe flourishing here, but not mine. Not like the others.

So I have refused to sow and now I reap the bitter emptiness. A stranger beside me hearing my old man's complaints when in another, better place I would be surrounded by stout sons, daughters ripe and fruitful as this teeming earth. I dread this season. For me, this peaceful rain is weeping.

You're correct. I've stayed on. Where else to go. And yes. She could have borne me children. Beautiful children, I believe. I've seen them in my dreams. The best of both of us combined in them. Yet so much stronger, so much more able and daring and full of life. But I knew my children would not grow up in the safe world I dreamed for them. I could not risk even the thought of watching them crushed in this upside-down world where we find ourselves. I couldn't bear the necessity of teaching them to live a lie. The lie required of us to live here under terms other people's lies demand.

Shame on me. Listen to me. Whining to a boy who strayed in out of the night.

No. No need to turn away. I did not mean to say you are a stranger still. You're much more. You abide my whining. I didn't know how deeply I missed another like myself beside me until you arrived. So many stories to tell. Too much bitter silence for too many years. Too much lost. I couldn't begin to talk, son, till I learned you were willing to listen.

Ha. There it is. My confession in a word. *Son.* Fathering you in my fancy. You know the tale. Old couple who'd given up hope of a child and one day the man finds a human cub in a wolf's den or a melon patch and brings it home to raise.

I owe my life to you.

Not me. She suckled you. I merely teach you to howl at the moon.

I'm not who I was when the storm dropped me here. The world's different. I'm different in it. You've taught me the shape of this different place.

It possesses no shape. Only a greedy tide rushing in, rushing out, washing everything away you've built when it was quiet, when you believed the waters would grant you peace, not come again.

But you are here. You remain.

We hide.

No. You are strong. You've built a place for yourselves. You have love. And each other. All I'm still searching for.

Listen to the rain. Listen closely, my friend. The storms in it, the rush of the tide. You can hear them plainly in each quiet, quiet, pattering footstep.

Many stories in the rain, I'm sure. You would tell one, I another. Though you said it makes you think of weeping, a soft, life-giving rain, nevertheless.

Once, in Stubbs' house in Horkstow, the country, I stood looking out at rain. Through a window on a landing on the stairs I had carried a horse up. The view gave onto a rolling meadow, a horizon of low gray hills in the distance. The meadow green, green as this one this morning. And in the field, a stand of huge oak trees soaked black by rain.

As I watched, the trees began to rise. Straight up. Slowly. Stately. Leaving the green earth. A cluster of trees like some gigantic, bristling man-of-war on invisible ropes lifted from the sea. I believed my eyes long enough to feel the wonder of what I was beholding. Trees floating, the solid earth left behind. Then I remembered rain. Saw the slants of it falling down. My eyes had mistaken the thing unmoving for the thing moving. Reversed the natural order. Downward was upward. What was rooted I saw free.

What moved I saw as still. A different world hidden in this one. A world that couldn't be, yet there it was in all its simple glory, being what it couldn't. My mistake no mistake at all. I look out now at these trees and remember they have the power to fly.

Have you ever considered the difficulty of painting rain. We see through it, but see it also as drops and slants and sheets. There and not there. Like the years I've spent in this land. A moment or an eternity. Here and not here.

I see myself in you. The whole business starting up again. Impatient, always racing to the finish. No time. All time. Rain transparent as the years. Nowhere, everywhere, escaping the canvas.

I thought I might spare you one last tale of a lying-in. Might spare myself the painful telling. But as you said, there are many stories in the rain. This one's in it this morning.

I'm in a cavelike room lit by many candles, whose flames shiver. Many other men crowded with me into this low-ceilinged, narrow, subterranean chamber. All the faces demon faces in the flickering darkness. Stubbs across the room, beside a sconce set low in the wall. When he leans closer to the shrouded table that separates us, his forehead a full-bellied white sail, the rest of his features smeared into the shadow of his beard. Crumbling head of a statue unearthed from ancient ruins.

Gentlemen, gentlemen. Your attention, please. Welcome to my humble shop. Though hardly attractive, it's perfectly suited to my business. You are all knowledgeable gentlemen. Each a scholar and master in his chosen field of endeavor. For the marvelous specimen I'm offering you this evening, each of you doubtless will have projects and plans. I guarantee you will not be disappointed by what you are about to see. So, gentlemen, without further ado, on with business.

You are truly a scoundrel, Krebs.

Shop, you say, Krebs. This dungeon and charnel house a shop.

Please, sirs. I am your humble servant. I claim no distinction of birth nor learning, none of the quality each of you gentlemen abundantly possesses. I earn my living as I must. Come, great sirs. Spare me. I am quite aware that such distinguished gentlemen have not gathered for the pleasure of my acquaintance. Yet mutual interest binds us, does it not. Or you wouldn't be here to bid for what I offer.

We'd dealt with Krebs before. One of the most unprincipled and successful of the resurrectionists. The stink of the grave clung to his ill-fitting clothes. Yet he comported himself like a fop. Fawning and simpering, he aped the manners and speech of his betters, all the while conveying an unquenchable arrogance. He harangued the men assembled in the cellar with a tone blending inextricably the flattery of imitation, the ridicule of mockery.

Behold. Behold.

With a flourish the pock-beaked, sparrow-shouldered grave robber flung back the shroud. A palpable gasp from the company at what he exposed. There on a kind of long, raised bench, the dark, naked body of a woman. African woman, belly swollen with child.

Perfect, is she not. Observe the symmetry, the delicate turn of limb. The flawless skin. A masterpiece, gentlemen. Eve. Helen of Troy. The ideal form of woman rendered in ebony.

Yes. Yes. Amazingly lifelike though dead a day and a half. Don't you wish you could breathe life into this lovely creature. Perhaps one of you can, good sirs. Perhaps she's not dead but enchanted by a witch. Awaits only the proper word, the proper touch, a kiss perhaps, to unseal her lips. One of you learned men may know the secret of restoring warmth and vitality to this perfect model of woman.

Do you not envy the man who inflated her belly. Observe how it slopes, a gentle hillock descending to the fleece-gated temple of Venus. In a few months the great mound might have detracted from her beauty, but frozen as it is, the roundness enhances. A fruit bursting with ripeness.

Purchase one, gentlemen, and you own two. The extraordinary female you see and the invisible freight she carries. A rare bargain, an especial treat to savor at your leisure. Whether you draw or dissect, whether you are a learned doctor of science or simply a curious soul dedicated to pursuing nature's secrets. In all my years in the trade I've never had the pleasure of offering a more interesting specimen. Observe its merits. I needn't waste precious time convincing gentlemen of such keen discernment how unique and valuable this treasure truly is.

You are my most valued customers. I'm grateful and loyal to all. To offer this marvel to one would be to deprive the others. Be fair, I said to myself. Let the gentlemen decide who shall have her. Thus in the name of fairness, rather than dealing with each of you in private, as is my usual custom, I have invited all my best friends here. She will go to the highest bidder.

Stubbs shrinks back from the table. From the brazen odiousness of the man. He detests him. Detests the bargaining, I know. Yet I understand Stubbs well enough to wager his eyes are fixed on the table. He'll hide himself in the shadows, yes. Hate auctioneer and auction, yes, but he'll bid. The prize irresistible. His imagination teeming already, daydreaming possibilities the African woman and child present for his art.

A stirring and buzz among the company. Insults shouted at

Krebs. Some gentlemen less shy than others close round the table. Inspecting, touching. Exchanging opinions, sighs, nervous laughter, lewd remarks.

It's not the same pain. Pain, yes. As any sensible creature feels pain. But surely not the same pain we feel, Stubbs. If it's the same pain, then we are monsters, aren't we. And we are not a nation of monsters.

Look here. The coarseness of hair, thickness of lips. A different sensibility betrayed by these different parts. I tended a black whore once. No Englishwoman could lie still and be handled as I handled her.

A professional numbness, sir. Consider the many gentlemen who would have purchased an interest in her private parts before you. Habit, sir.

I disagree. A dullness. A difference. They do not buck and mewl in childbirth like your common English wench. Oh, one or two will, those who have been spoiled by too much familiarity with the habits of their mistresses. They are like the wild Indians of North America, who I'm told go off alone in the woods to drop their foals. No tears. No wringing of hands and screeching for Heaven's aid.

Excuse me, sir. You are wrong, wrong, wrong. I've cut them open. Unpacked the organs one by one. No difference beneath the skin.

How can you deny the evidence of your eyes. The dark folds. Plumpness of bottom. The Hottentot women store victuals there like camels store water. Trek the wilderness for weeks without eating. And here. A laxness. A drooping porch so the whelp slides out easily, painlessly.

This single specimen proves nothing. If the only Irishman a

Hottentot ever saw was red-haired and six foot high, would the black bugger be correct to surmise all Irishmen tall and ruddy.

I retreated from the voices till I felt cobwebs brush my head, a cold wall against my back. Wished I could turn to stone. Wished I could take her place on the slab. Give her my warm flesh and blood.

My legs trembled. I pressed my hands into the wall. I needed the stones for support. Needed their roughness cutting into my skin. The African woman on the table was my sister, mother, daughter. I slept inside her dark stomach. I was gripping her heart with both my hands and it was the world's heart, hard and cold as ice. She'd been stolen from me and now I was about to lose her again. Knives would slice her open, hack her to bits. They'd find me cowering in the black cave of her womb again, dead and alive, alive and dead. I wished for the fiery breath of a dragon, for tongues of flame to leap from my mouth and consume that terrible cellar where the auctioneer had already begun his obscene chant.

Liam was up and out first that October morning as always. October days can belong to any season, contain all seasons in a single span of twenty-four hours. Summer sunshine and fall chill. A hint of winter before the sun rises and after it sets, or when you step from bright sunlight into deep shade. Winter in gusting winds from the west. Spring in the colorful, urgent preparations of growing things to change their shape. Dying leaves in flames. Clamor of wild geese honking, a din belying the disciplined formation of their sweep across the sky.

Liam always rises first. Stealthy as a ghost, he sets the house in order. I've learned to wait until he leaves, then it's my turn to warm my hands at his fire, drink tea he's brewed, tend chores he's assigned me, pick up tools he's laid out, join him at the work site he's chosen for the day.

She waits till I'm gone from the house before she stirs. I doubt she's asleep while I putter about. I think I hear her listening, listening. Both of us, while we lie abed, unsure whether we're alive or dead, using the sound of Liam to confirm the pulse within us.

I was about to depart that morning for the fields when she called out. Her voice startled me. I was used to quiet at this dawn-ish hour, neither night nor day. She had entered my thoughts, of course, long before I heard her voice. Every morning I listen for her listening. Teaching myself the shape, the texture of her listening, how it changes the silence. I wonder what her first thoughts are. Do the years fall away each night. Is she a child again, curled in the dark hollow of herself. How many women in her bed. Which one will she be when she opens her eyes.

Does she ever ask herself what I might be thinking. Could she hear me listening for her listening. Hear my soundless addresses to Liam. Question after question in the quiet of morning. About both these people, man and woman, who had taken me into their home. In their odd manner both befriended me. Both talked to me, told me stories about their lives, but would I ever be more than a stranger passing through.

Come here, to the bed, please, and bring the salve . . .

Weeks before at the edges of the yard I'd been chopping weeds when she'd sat Liam on a stump and rubbed the musky-scented salve into his back. She'd scooped a measure with the fingers of one hand, set down the jar, replaced the stopper, rubbed her hands till both palms glistened, then applied the stuff in long, forceful strokes, his flesh a medium into which she plunges and swims.

Finishing, she had pushed up the sleeves of her smock, wiped her fingers on her bare arms. That warm spring day she'd glanced up at me once while she'd worked on him. Perhaps the notion of summoning me to take a turn on the stump had crossed her mind. If it did, nothing came of it. I had continued to chop and rake while she oiled Liam's lean back, his shoulders and neck.

The rubbing salve from the cupboard shelf.

Good morning, madam. God be with you this beautiful morning.

Her eyes meet him from the bed. She's been awake for hours, the eyes say. We never sleep, they say. They say they know everything from birth to death about him.

I see you found it. Thank you and good morning to you, sir.

May I fetch you tea before I go.

No. I want you to stay. I need your blessing this morning, boy preacher. Pray for my aching old woman's back. Pray by dipping your fingers in the jar. Pray by applying your hands to the soreness that seems this morning even more ancient and unforgiving than I am.

Spread salve on your hands. Not much. It's strong. Then rub it in. Not gently, sir. Start at my neck. Lean your weight into it. Old pains. Old bones. Old sins deep inside my flesh you must pray vigorously to ease.

Beg pardon, madam, but I'm awaited. The south field. We're haying it today.

Liam won't wait. He'll begin without you and once begun won't notice you're missing. I claim your hands a few minutes this morning. He can sweat you the rest of the day.

She sits up in the bed. Briskly the shift is yanked over her head, tossed away. Pale flash of thick-nippled breasts. Her hips twist under the blanket as she flops onto her stomach. Reaching behind herself, she pushes the covers down past her waist, then her thin arms reach up, gather her hair and part it. A sheaf in each fist she lifts off her shoulders and lets fall, one on either side to bare her neck.

You see the poor clay you must revive. Pray hard, then you may be on your way.

Why is he repeating excuses, saying no to himself even as his fingers unstopper the earthen jar, even as he cups his hand to be smeared with what his fingers dig out. An odor rises from the jar, almost harsh, many odors compounded into one, more pleasant than unpleasant when, rather than shying away, he lets himself breathe it, search it. He coats his fingertips, brings them closer to his nose. Mud in it and meat frying, honey, wet pine needles flooring the forest, sage, black leaves moldering at the bottom of a pile returning to soil, mint, blue sleeves, applerot, this woman's scents collecting at the cavemouths and hollows of her body while she sleeps, the bread smell of her skin warmed all night beneath the bedclothes.

Whiteness of the seam above her neck where the hair has been pulled aside shocks him. He would have thought of her back as a white woman's naked back except for this whiter, barer strip of skull bedding the mottled roots of her hair. He was afraid to touch the seam. Rested his thumbs just below it, letting his fingers circle the column of her neck. Touching, tightening. Gently kneading.

Too delicate, sir. Lean into it. Yes. Lean. Better.

Here she was finally under his hands. Liam's red-haired white woman. Her skin white, his black. Disguises. Worn so long nobody remembers they are disguises. A masquerade. In costume nothing they do to each other counts. Black or white. Both of them unreal. White and black. Evil dreams of power. Could he crush this white woman under his hands, no tears, no blood. Is anyone telling the truth.

Is the only thing that counts what you can get away with. White or black. Stealing, lying, pretending.

She's quiet under his hands. He studies her. Not a white woman's back. White was the colorlessness of her exposed skull, the seam the sun never touched. Against her pale skin his fingers darker, a darkness as far from black as her flesh from white. Who had named the difference black or white. She wasn't a white woman. Her skin variously tinted and grained. A shower of petals freckled her shoulders. Subtle blushes of red, gold, blue, soft in the early morning light. He remembers the pearly interior of a charm an old slave woman had held out to him. On a string round her neck, a shell with the sea's voice inside. Many-chambered and whorled like an ear, its insides partly outside, a pink gash until you looked closer, then, like this woman's skin, the shell a wash of many faint colors, nameless shades scrolling one into the other.

Don't daydream, boy preacher. Exhort. These old bones need a fiery sermon this morning.

Beneath his hands she's surprisingly firm. A muscular resistance. Echo of Liam's sinewy body. He discovered the smaller, compact woman she'd become, inside skin that couldn't shrink quite fast enough to fit.

As he rubbed her back, he was peeling layers. He was past the linen shift. The nakedness. The whiteness. The scrimshaw lines of age decorating her skin. Were his fingers finding what Liam yearned to paint, what he himself had wished he could preach one day.

Was he near the last layer of her. Could he reach the core beneath. Why does the question excite him. Should he risk going further. Risk losing her.

If he pushed deeper, would he change her, change himself. Would she let him. Black and white gone. What came next. He thinks of how it might feel to see her with Liam's eyes. Just a glimmer of the idea, without thinking further to where it might lead, enough to dissolve his edges, threaten the borders of the figure he draws in his mind when he speaks his name, says *me, myself, I*.

He sees Liam working, work at Liam's steady, unstinting pace, to construct a woman from this hair and meat and bone. Liam's hand in what's present and absent in her, the windows of her green eyes, the holes and folds and hollows of her that are porches, doors, stairways, rooms, the clearing surrounded by woods, the raked earth into which her foundations sink, the fences, gardens, meadows you see approaching her as Liam does, drained from working the land, sun at his back sinking red in the west, his weariness, his desire something he will spread like rugs on the plank floor of her, everything she's heard and forgotten, the ghosts swarming in this dwelling of her Liam has sawn and split the raw timber for, chosen a site, roofed with cedar shakes, driven in the precious nails.

When he looks down and sees her as a place where Liam's sweat and toil are no longer separate from hers but are this edifice, this body where two people live and are dying, there is no room therein for him to hide and he's ashamed of his trespass, cringes from the idea of beholding her through Liam's eyes. No, no, he says. Did she hear him. If no one heard him, could he chase the thought away. As if there had been no thought. No history.

Lost in Liam's eyes, he loses her. Loses the map of her he's opening. Is she white again. After the map tells him where he is, why couldn't he carefully refold it along its ancient creases and return it precisely to the spot where he'd discovered it.

Has she fallen asleep. He's sitting beside her, his shadow, one hand on the bed, the other hand stroking, pressing the base of her spine. He remembers a fire, an old woman undressing before it. The sad wilt of her buttocks into the tops of her thighs. The woman shedding years as she crosses the room, a slim girl when she steps into the tub. If he raised the blanket hiding her hips, which woman would he discover. Rubbing and kneading, tracing the long knobby bone with his fingers, he believes he'd find both, the mystery of both, both and more in this month whose days contain all seasons, this dawn quiet as the other he is recalling, a dawn to which they both return, strangers, lovers, as he stretches to touch the naked foot that has poked its way from under the covers.

When I looked up, the night sky so black, black, the big stars looming, I knew I must be in the Africa of Liam's stories. I was the boy he'd been before he was snatched away forever. His country big enough to hold England in its palm, his old world dwarfing even the immensity of this raw new one to which he'd run with his dreams, his flame-haired white woman. Each star a whirling note of music, a drumbeat I was almost close enough to hear.

Lying on my back in a field, I tried to make my body rise. I knew it could. Prayed it would. My body often strayed. A trick of the mind. The power of my spirit to detach itself, rising immaterial and curious, gazing down at the solid flesh and bones.

While I prayed for my body to rise, a terrible loneliness assailed me. One day my body would desert me and I'd be a ghost rooted to nothing, roaming aimlessly forever unless my body returned. Beneath that African sky I tried to will my body to rise, rise closer to the energy uncoiling from the stars, the circles within circles within circles nearly reaching me, almost audible. If my body would take me just a little bit higher, I'd hear the song, become part of it, the stars, that blackness over my head.

As I lay there wondering why it was so hard to will my body to perform a simple trick it had managed many times effortlessly on its own, wondering why there were so many things in the world and beyond the world and I was only one of them, could never be another, none of them but the one I was, yearning, wondering what sound each star held, wondering if all together they made harmonious music or if in the black night sky each one sang lonely and separate as the many things of this earth must sing until the day the broken kingdom is restored, I remembered the dream. The dream she'd whispered coming to me that night. Loving me that night. Old woman, girl, black, white. Bald, fiery-haired. The dream of the African girl who'd told the people they must kill their cattle.

She was the daughter of a priest. Perhaps her mother one of the many wives of the wizard father Liam had left behind in Africa. In the dream she weeps. *My child. My child,* a refrain mingled with her sobs. I think she is mourning a lost child until our eyes meet, and I know I'm the child.

She says her name and the letters of it print crookedly in the air, hang like a tilted shop sign. *Nongqawuse.* She is these letters, the letters would be her, ever after.

Then she sings me inside her dream:

We lived by the sea, but we didn't love the sea and neither did the sea love us. We did not swim in the hostile saltwater. To eat its scaly, slippery creatures was an abomination. We were people of cattle. The cattle were the people, the people the cattle. We drank the milk and blood of our beasts, named them as carefully, hopefully, as we named our children. Cattle God's gift to us, our past and future secured by His blessing.

Along the edges of the ever restless sea, in deep black pools of sweet water where nothing moves but reeds nodding in the wind, time began. These pools, the elders say, are black throats swallowing the rivers that race down from the mountains. There is no bottom to these pools, the clear mountain water flows to the belly of God, who is never sated. Nourishing His vastness stretched under the land. Golden beaches and soft green plains, the ripe foothills, the blue mountains scraping the moon, all rest on Him. When He belches, thunder rumbles, lightning is the blink of His eye. His piss life-giving rain filling the rivers that empty into the dark mouths of the pools.

Though we feared its roar, its ceaseless heaving, the sea also protected us. Until the day it brought the whites.

We welcomed them. We did not understand they had come to murder us and steal our land. When we learned their evil plan, we fought them, but their gods were too strong. The whites banished us from our lands, stole our cattle, brought great woe and misery to the people. A terrible sickness swept the countryside, killing our herds. We who had been powerful upon the land were starving beggars. Our chiefs could not lead, our warriors could not fight, our women deserted their children, our young men began to worship alien gods. We looked to the pale people from across the sea to deliver us from the destruction they had wrought.

On one of those sad days during the season of death, days of a sorrow so far beyond sorrow we had no name for it, I was bathing with my sister in a pool at the edge of the land, one of the black pools deep and calm as palm wine in its gourd of boulders that protects it from the sea. Weakened by hunger, we had stumbled and crawled through the thorn bushes to this place of refuge, hoping the ancient waters might soothe us, save us.

The sea's roar allowed strangers to approach. We didn't hear them behind us till one spoke. My sister bolted like a wounded antelope. Splashing out of the water, she ran limping toward our village, screaming for help.

I could not stir. Afraid to look at the strangers, I stared down into the dark water, watched it restore itself, close tightly again around my knees, my image locked there, perfect double of a young girl too affrighted to speak or move.

Listen to me, daughter, and do not be afraid, a voice said. We are your father's brothers. You've heard the people say our names.

He said the names and I knew them and his voice was kind, but still I dared not raise my eyes to look upon his face.

Listen with all your ears, child. You must carry my message to our people. Tell them the plague destroying their herds is God's curse upon those who have forsaken His ways. Tell them we must return to the old ways. The sacred path the ancestors walked. But first the people must kill their cattle.

Spread my message to all the clans, daughter. Bid them hear me well. This evil world is dying. A new one on its way. The whites will be driven out. The ancestors will return and dwell again on the earth, bringing with them endless herds of cattle to fill our kraals.

But only those who kill all their cattle will be welcomed in this new world. The people must kill their cattle now if they wish to live forever in peace and harmony when the ancestors return.

Hear me, child. Instruct the people to kill their cattle. It is the only way to save themselves when this evil world ends.

No one believed my story. Men from the village hurried to the pool with my sister and found no one there but me. Found only the quiet black pools, the stillness of time never-ending, waiting to begin.

They threatened to beat us. Accused us of lying. Called us silly girls. Though a few heard truth in the prophecy, most scoffed. The cattle are the people. The people the cattle, the elders said. To kill our cattle, they said, would be to kill ourselves. What devil has taught this child a terrible lie.

But death reigned everywhere. War, famine and disease left the survivors dazed and without hope. More of the people began to believe the prophecy. It swept like wildfire across a parched veldt.

Though the prophecy promised paradise, a terrible future lived in the words. They were a mouth eating the people. When we slaughtered our herds, we doomed our children.

We'd been deceived. It was not the shade of my father's brother who spoke through me that day beside the pool. No. It was a spirit of despair grown strong inside our breasts, as the whites had grown strong in our land, during years of fighting and plague and hate. A spirit who whispered the lies of the invaders in our ears. Who tricked us into toiling for our foes. Taught us to kill our cattle, murder ourselves.

Beware, she said. Beware. Beware. Do not kill your cattle. Do not speak with your enemy's tongue. Do not fall asleep in your enemy's dream.

Tears fill her eyes. Her grief is mine. I weep with her. Afraid to waken and find her gone. Afraid if I don't awaken, I'll become the weeping and perish.

She sees me trembling. Her arms circle me. Fear not, she says. She says she's only a spirit in a dream, a dream like the prophecy she preached to her people, a dream like the new day the false prophecy had promised, the day when the whites would be swept from the land, the dead return, the cattle plentiful again as nodding grasses in the meadows above the sea, a dream, a dream, my child.

Sleep, my child, my pumpkin, and I will come to you in another dream. This one is too old and sad, she said. I will return in a happier dream in a new land where the cattle are not dying, the children not dying. Only our enemies dead in the new dream, the slaughter of our cattle, the slaughter of our children not dyeing our hands blood red with guilt. A love dream. Yours. Mine.

When I awakened I was covered in sweat. Naked on the grass under that starry African sky. The scents of her body mixed with mine. A smell I recognized and have never forgotten. My seed hot and sticky on my loins. The stars howling. The taste of ashes on my lips. Then the acrid odor of smoke, smoke's burn in my eyes.

From where I lay on a bed of tall grasses pressed under my body, I could see Liam's house burning. A torch flaming at the crest of the slope down which I'd paced earlier that sultry night to sleep under the stars. A torch with five tongues of flame licking the black sky. One for Liam, one for her. One for the ghost of me that died with them. One for the children they did not dare to breed, the children they feared exposing to the madness. The other tongue of flame for Liam's African brethren ripped with him from the land of their fathers to preach false prophecies.

Liam was wrong. The town had not forgotten them. White

woman, black man. No. The townsfolk were patient, cunning, treacherous, unforgiving. This was a final reckoning of the peculiar arithmetic.

How many of my little congregation at Radnor survived the night of terror I never learned. I must have survived, I'm here telling the tale, but sometimes I wonder.

You ask me why the whites attacked their colored neighbors. Why a night of rape and murder and fire. I didn't know then, nor do I know now. Except then I believed an answer might exist, believed I might learn it and learning it might make some difference next time. So I went to Philadelphia to fight the plague, to purge myself of hate, to find you.

I found in that city of brotherly love the country of sickness and dying the African woman's dream foretold. And Philadelphia was a prophecy of other cities to come, as my stay in the village of Radnor had been prophecy and fulfillment of the city.

Circles within circles. Expanding and contracting at once — boundless, tight as a noose. God's throat, belly, penis, cunt, asshole, the same black ditch. The people an unbroken chain of sausages fed in one end and pulled out the other. A circle without and within, the monstrous python swallowing itself, birthing its tail.

PART TWO

But I will stretch out my hand against the prophets
who have false visions and who foretell lies.

EZEKIEL 13:22

Just as I sit beside you on this bed, speaking to you, the dead speak to me. I feel them as the song says drawing me on, drawing me on. I found Philadelphia, of course. Fought the fever. Met Richard Allen. Old Bishop Allen, dead now, but I see him, he sits on the side of his bed, head bowed, wondering if his God will follow him and Absalom Jones and their flock of dark sheep into the church they are building. Allen is struck — nay, dumbfounded — by the audacity of the task he's undertaken. No one can help him now. Not Absalom Jones. Not the men and women who have placed their faith entire in him. Though his God is everywhere, sees everything, He's chosen to disappear into the quiet, somber chill of Bishop Allen's bedchamber.

The weight and pinch of Allen's heavy body bears down on the bed's wooden railing. His haunches spread. Pumpkin-colored feet protrude where he stares down past the nightshirt stretched over his knees. Weighty flesh, its liquids and stenches, the rot and sting of its hungers. He shuts his eyes to escape the room, the relentless complaints of his aging body.

He breathes slowly, an eternity between breaths, space for the body to be undone and tumble backward through its many births, the mothers, continents, seas, backward to the stillness of stone, the mud beneath stone that had never dreamed the light he closes his eyes against in this room in Philadelphia, light from one stubby candle in a dish of clay beside his bed.

Father. Father. The enormity of what he set in motion when he led his brethren from the white people's church engulfs him. A mantle of mourning, and he hadn't guessed till this moment the full burden on his shoulders. God had dwelt in the white people's church. Leaving it, he'd turned his back on God. With Satan's pride and scheming arrogance he'd gathered other rebels around him, multiplied his own sin by leading them away from God's house.

God's house even though the whites had profaned it. He'd never felt God's presence in their church more surely than the morning the deacons of St. George's had ordered him up off his knees, back into a corner of a gallery they'd decided to assign to him and others like him, whose skin, the deacons said, bore the mark of Cain. He'd pitied the church elders. They'd changed shape before his eyes, transformed by the evil clouding their hearts as they laid hands on him and his brethren at prayer. He was ashamed for them, the stewards of the church, his neighbors, men whose names he knew, men whose wives and children watched from the front pews as their men marched among us, disturbing the sanctity of our prayers, attempting to herd us into a corner, separate us from our fellow parishioners, treating us as if they didn't know us, our names, our families. As if they'd never heard God's commandments forbidding the outrage they were committing.

He needed God then. To show him why he shouldn't strike back, resist with all the strength in his body the evil of men forcing themselves betwixt him and his faith.

He needed God as counterweight to balance the evil of what was transpiring in the church. He saw fear in dark faces. Hate in white. The confusion of the children, the helplessness of a few faces unable to be either black or white if it meant they must act out the role to which their color doomed them. He needed God somewhere, somehow keeping track, weaving the ugliness of what was happening into some larger pattern, a tapestry whose myriad scenes he might never grasp but whose overarching design promised that God's hand was active in this, even this.

And what he'd needed had shone forth. A kind of lightness, giddiness when he'd risen to his feet from the boards of the church floor. A whispering in his ear. Yes. Yes. Lightness but also iron. His voice didn't tremble when he spoke to his brethren. He unclenched his fists, his heart. Now *he* was standing, touching people's shoulders, nudging, hugging, guiding, gathering, moving the others in a body, not to some shameful margin but out the church door, heads held higher than when they'd entered.

Yes. God was there. A rock he'd leaned on. Pushed into a corner by evil, the power of evil rampant, he'd found that the seeming absence of God was God's best proof. The pang of needing Him, the prospect of a world without Him, evil pressing down, no light, no hope, the impossibility of coping in such a world, where evil has the power to consume you, to consume the world — that pang of urgent need and utter desolation, that stab in the heart, reveals Him.

God surely there in the building white people had erected. His love imminent in the dumb, humble things of wood and tallow and cloth, even as His presence turns water to wine, wine to blood, changes minutes and hours spent inside the church to time without beginning or end. Yet in his stiff-necked pride he'd led his people away from a holy abode of grace. Away from Canaan, back into the wilderness from which God had brought them safely out. Away from an ark of safety into what. An unhallowed, unpaid-for house, so hastily constructed the green lumber of the benches sweats pitch.

Allen sat on the edge of his bed thinking these thoughts and might be sitting still except he heard a voice telling him something like a story.

You cannot lead, Allen, unless you turn your back on God's house. Unless you promise to deliver to the others what in your pride you saw fit to seek for yourself — a new beginning, a new tabernacle where the holy presence you deserted will reappear. Faith, Allen. The step into darkness, the leap. The others believed you, amened you, pledged to follow you, and now you cower in this gloomy chamber, sorry for yourself, frightened in the depths of your soul as you consider a simple truth. Is truth so unbearable. Are you uncertain now of your goal. Speak your fear aloud, Allen: will God indeed accompany you to this new house of worship you are abuilding.

In your anger, your fervor (or was it vanity, Allen, phrase-making, a desire to be praised even when you know you don't deserve it — the need to be viewed as a certain kind of man in spite of the fact you know you are not such a man), you never doubted you were sinned against when they tried to pen you like goats in the church's rear gallery, nor doubted that God would follow you and those others if you deserted St. George's. In the righteousness of your grievance, the mean hypocrisy of the deacons, no ambiguity lurked. The actions of the church elders mocked God. You sought only justice, fairness, no more nor less than the church was obliged to suffer you, unless it dishonored its covenant with the Almighty.

When you marched out, marched away, admit, Allen, in your secret heart you hoped the entire congregation, black and white, would rise and march with you in affirmation of God's law, the holy community of His Word. Then the procession would not have ended in some sticky green place but would have danced along the Philadelphia streets like a cleansing wind. When you arrived again at the sacred portal through which you had departed, swelled now to a multitude by the spirit no one could resist, you would pack the church, send up glad hosannas of great joy resounding in every corner of the land.

Pleasing perhaps even to God's ear, to His eye, as you knelt to thank Him for sundering us one from the other, black from white, rich from poor, man from woman, age from youth, so we might find ourselves, finally, so gloriously conjoined once more. As He intended. All creation worshiping Him, one flesh, under one roof.

The voice, the bright vision fades, Allen is alone again, an old man on his knees. God's absence confirmed by evil everywhere raging. The need.

He'd slid from the edge of the bed like some soulless cluster of dirt and stones loosed from a hillside when the earth shivers. Yes. His flock will gather at the new building, a blacksmith's shed horses had hauled to a vacant lot. But does he have the power to summon God. Do they. God promised him nothing. Yet Allen had coaxed his African brethren, prodded, enticed, harangued them as if surely, surely God would be waiting when they crossed over to the promised land.

In the darkness, the quiet of the room (pumpkin breath wheezing, part of the quiet, the figure against which the ground of quiet defines itself), he wishes to be a white man. Holds the wish long enough for it to become a wet intimacy his tongue traces inside his pursed mouth, inside his lower lip, against his teeth, the sour, vacant spaces where teeth once rooted. A wish he would whisper aloud — *wouldn't you be one of them if you could* — as a half-serious question to someone in the room, if there were someone he could trust, someone who could smile coldly, understand, nod, never say anything to anyone about the bishop's confession. If that's what the thought was.

The thought curdles, a foulness up from his gut, compressed in his throat. He expels it, a hissing jet that buckles the candle flame, nearly extinguishing it. He stares at the pale, wrinkled stub, the mincing yellow tip.

He despises his duplicity. Despises the cowardice bringing him low. To this shameful impasse. A frightened soul begging for certainty, for supernatural assurance and signs. He would walk in God's way. He would be a warrior in the Lord's army, yet he holds back from the fray, petitions God to storm ahead, banners flying, clearing the field of enemies, of peril. He's prepared to sacrifice, to commit himself and his people to battle, but he's waiting for the clear blast of God's trumpet to lead him.

In his heart he does not wish to be white, to be one of them. He's the man he is. Not some other. Yet he is praying for an easier way than the way opening up for him. Why has he been orphaned in this strange land, in this unimaginable city. Divided first from others, then from himself. A wound he inflicts upon himself, a wound he cannot heal himself. He does not secretly yearn to be one of the whites. No. No. He is praying for a lifting of the burden that crushes them all, black and white, in their tortured, bitter dealings one with the other. He cannot change what he is and they cannot change what they are, and he cannot pray to God to wipe white people off the face of the earth and also keep his heart free for Christ's mercy, Christ's love, so he is not wishing to be white, but if he calls on Heaven to purge whatever it is the whites fear and hate in him, must it also be a prayer for sweet annihilation.

He hears the mighty pounding of waves. On both sides of him like a million million rearing horses the sea curls back, white underbelly and flashing green hooves, the roar and menace in check as he stands on a dry highway between steep canyon walls of churning water. God's will has opened this path through the sea and planted him here as a pilgrim, as witness, pioneer and point man, and he must summon his brethren to follow him, to trust this strait, dry, narrow way, but mist blinds, the sting of salt spray, the shrieking gulls, thunder of ponderous waves slamming against the thin air restraining them. He is perplexed, frightened, stunned by the tumult. Though his feet are on dry land and the miracle that brought him this far is undeniable, he falters, begs for a vision of the new world at the far end of this threatening path — the earth restored, flood receded, peace.

Like Lot's wife, he is doomed if he turns around. With the eyes in back of his head he counts his people, names them, the meager column of African folk, women, men, children exiting through the church door. He shouts to send his voice above the roaring of furious waves. His people are behind him. If he doubts, if he halts again, the stony waters will come crashing down with the force of mountains.

He cannot hold the posture of prayer. He will not beg. He will not grovel. He will not forget what brought him to his resolve. Unwieldy saddles of meat, the groaning bones and grinding joints collapsed in a heap beside the bed, he must refashion into a man. He is no thing of clay waiting for a spirit's breath. He must rise on his own two feet. Arise and go. Where, Allen. Where.

◇   ◇   ◇

Philadelphia, 18 January 1793

Dearest,

A new year has dawned. I'm sure you are happy, positively aglow as always in the bosom of your family. Remember you are there on loan only. I count the hours till your return to the city.

Yesterday I witnessed a sublime event. From the yard of the Walnut Street jail the Frenchman Blanchard ascended in a hot-air balloon. A mob of 40,000 including the noble General Washington himself cheered the exciting launch.

At my urging, Monsieur Blanchard graciously consented to conduct an experiment aboard his aerial vessel. I suggested that he carry a helper in the gondola, a steward to attend his needs and measure with a pulse glass the blood's response to the pure, thin air of great elevation. As you share my compassion for their misunderstood race, you will be tickled to learn that a Negro fellow, my suggestion also, accompanied the Frenchman on his daring voyage. Who better to perform the duties of steward than one whose natural inclination is to serve and please; and whose blood better than the Negroes', with its tropical lushness and excitability, to record the heart's fluctuations as the balloon rose.

Men flying like birds. The commencement of an *anno mirabi-*

lus, no doubt. Perhaps mere spectacle and amusement today, but what marvelous, undreamed possibilities for the future. The first command to man, *subdue the earth*, like every other divine command must be fulfilled. Dry land and water have long ago yielded to man's dominion and it remains for him only to render air subservient to his will.

I believe this balloon and other ingenious inventions open boundless prospects for our new nation in the coming century.

Closer to humble hearth and home, for us earth-huggers the New Year appears just as bright with promise. Your health is returning, my practice thriving, the city growing and prosperous; my civic and scientific projects, including the hobbyhorse of a separate Negro church, daily receive more encouragement.

At the gala dinner tonight I expect to learn from Monsieur Blanchard the results of the pulse glass business. Soon, soon, in your lovely presence, I shall unburden myself of that news and much, much more.

❖   ❖   ❖

I cannot see the words I would write in this book, nor see the book, nor see the world the words would venture to describe — I depend upon another's hand to set down my thoughts — I must open to another my most private spaces — my wishes, disappointments, dreams, what is never spoken except in conversation inside my own poor head — what I say when no one is listening — what I might say if someone dear consented to listen — what I say when I wish only God to hear.

What I cannot nor would not utter to another and can barely

write in secret to myself I must lay bare in this book, because there is no other way to maintain a record — I must expose my heart and soul to my maid Kathryn — so be it.

I love Kate — *she owns* — I take her free hand in mine — tell her not to stop writing with the other — dear Kate, you must learn to speak my heart — a task fitting and proper because you, Kate, truly reside inside my breast — a second tender tremor there.

While your hand was stilled upon the page I caressed it — your dark hand under mine — my hand slightly larger and heavier — yet not nearly as strong, though my Kathryn's bones are light as a bird's — a sisterly likeness — the same texture of flesh, same short, blunt fingers — fine articulation of vein and bone beneath the skin — slim palm and narrowness of wrist — more alike than different in this unbroken night where glorious vision no more reigns — her dark color and my lack of one indistinguishable by touch. *My flesh moans, why can't you hear it.*

I depend on you, dear Kate, in this writing business as in so much else — your arm to guide — your ear to listen — your eyes to see — depend on you to write my words and then read them back to me so I may pick up the thread of my wanderings — depend upon you as Daedalus depended on the golden cord fastened round his waist to rescue him from the dread Minotaur's labyrinth, as the wizard's son Icarus depended on the wings his father contrived to visit the realm of soaring eagles.

I entreat the goddess Clio to bless my efforts on these pages — Clio's lamp and your kind arm, my Kate — may they guide me through the vast gallery where memories hang — paintings on its walls — arm in arm may we stroll the winding corridors — together we shall step into first one frame, then another — moments return — the pictures are alive — each a teeming eastern bazaar — unfurling like luxurious tapestries merchants shake out to tempt our purchase — we smile and pass on — to the turbaned juggler with a great curved sword in his mouth — the blur of his hands tossing flaming torches high over our heads — a fiery wheel turning in the air — a universe within each of the paintings we encounter in the gallery — unexpected smells and sights and sounds abound — wonders in each picture that from a distance had appeared to be only a frozen splash of color.

But I grow too fanciful — who keeps this gallery where invisible artists display their handiwork to viewers who have no eyes.

As I embark upon this writing business, I promise to be serious as a miser counting his hoard — each morning after I dispatch the servants to their chores, after I have kissed and said good morning to Dr. Thrush, who doubtless since dawn will have been ensconced in his study, attending to the never-ending duties of his calling — before I breakfast — content with the pot of tea, you, sweet Kathryn, carry to my bedroom — as near then to first as I can manage, I shall attend to my book — and you, my little book, pray treat me as a doting suitor or loving parent would — indulge with smiles the ordinariness of my thoughts and secrets.

You too, Kathryn, must practice patience as I stumble in these pages before I learn to walk — I intend these scribblings as a private record — never any eye but mine must view them — and since my eyes are blind, only yours, Kathryn — yours that are mine — must ever look upon my words — you know my heart in this matter — your silence my license.

That settled, pray, indulge my prattle — my digressions — my shamelessness — I refuse to compose as if a brace of scholars or clerics or gossiping matrons observe over my shoulder — pledge to speak only truth here — as I learn truth — as this book perhaps will teach me better to discern it.

I trust you, dearest Kate, to record exactly the spill of my thoughts — slow me if I speak too rapidly — ask me to repeat words you miss — but please, judge not — censor not — whether you recall a matter differently or not at all or wish me to cease because you believe enough has been said or more than enough said or said previously or not said well — you must be my unprotesting pen — let my heart guide you.

Attend me when my words are not sweet and harmonious — not nectar flowing but words buzzing and stinging like angry bees — dragon's teeth sown in your innocent soil, my journal.

Whatever befalls — we are launched — little book, you and I and Kate — I trust you both with my life — come, my friend — sister — swear one last time you will hear and bear everything I dictate to you — promise never to speak it to another soul — let us seal our bargain with a kiss.

❖   ❖   ❖

Philadelphia, 22 August 1793

Dearest

This day agreeably to invitation I dined a mile from town, under the shade of several large trees, with about a hundred carpenters and others who met to celebrate the raising of the roof of the African church. They forced me to take the head of the table, much against my inclinations. The dinner was plentiful — the liquors were of the first quality — and the dessert, which consisted only of melons, was very good. We were waited upon by nearly an equal number of black people. I gave them the two following toasts: "Peace on earth and good will to men" and "May African churches everywhere soon succeed to African bondage." After which we rose, and the black people (men and women) took our seats. Six of the most respectable of the white company waited upon them, while Mr. Nicholson, myself and two others were requested to set down with them, which we did, much to the satisfaction of the poor blacks.

Never did I witness such a scene of innocent — nay, more, such virtuous and philanthropic joy. Billy Grey in attempting to express his feelings to us was checked by a flood of tears. After they had dined, they all came up to Mr. Nicholson and took him by the hand, and thanked him for his loan of money to them. One of them, an old man whom I did not know, addressed him in the following striking language: "May you live long, sir, and when you die, may you not die eternally." The company broke up and came to town about six o'clock in good order, few or perhaps none of them having drunken more than three or four glasses of wine. To me it will be a day to be remembered with pleasure as long as I live.

❖   ❖   ❖

Who's there.

He stands, shivering, underdressed for the bite of November wind, hat in hand, the city cap he's taken to wearing, for reasons he'd be hard pressed to explain, since his arrival in Philadelphia. Just inside the doorway of the paneled entry hall on the very square of parquet floor where the young female servant who'd answered his knock had left him. Dark wood, polished to a watery gleam, surrounds him. Portraits in gilded frames. One smaller, japanned frame, oval-shaped, that does not contain a painting of a face but a mirror rounded like an eyeball or belly or teardrop. It reflects an image of this space in which he stands, the hall and himself in the hall, as if poured from a great distance, spreading over the glass's convex surface. His face distorted there as it had been on the back of spoons he'd polished for his master's table. He leans closer to the glass, the hallway disappears. His grotesquely enlarged head and leering eye fill the mirror. His eye transformed into a giant fish swallowing him.

He thinks he's alone in the hallway, affixed to his square on the checkerboard floor till he hears her voice *Who's there.*

He hadn't expected a woman. And two already had surprised him. The comely African servant girl who'd answered his knock. This one's *who's there* catching him staring at himself in the trick bubble of glass. She'd glided soundless into the hallway, twenty feet away. Her arms hover at her sides, poised just above the green-striped pockets of her lavender gown.

His errand difficult enough without surprises. Without a white woman's challenge to identify himself, a black woman's soft dark eyes. He'd practiced what he'd say if spoken to by the white man who owned this grand house. A man who held in his hands the power of life and death over the city's entire African community. Sitting in his room over the Hart and Hare, he'd imagined the imperious torrent of the man's words overwhelming him. Himself tongue-tied in the man's presence. How would he inject his own spare, measured responses. And what dread weight might attach, if any weight at all, to his simple answers to simple questions.

He'd played both roles. The aristocratic white doctor who in the years since his return from study in England had stormed to the leadership of the city's medical fraternity. A brilliant, brash, handsome man who they say is impatient with fools, full of himself, perhaps to the point of arrogance, yet a fair and decent sort at bottom, so the stories go. Polite to the lower orders — merchants, tradesmen, mechanics, respectful even toward the African people, if rumor and Bishop Allen's assurances briefing him for this urgent mission could be depended upon. Impeccable manners and deportment, an elegant dresser, a biting, rakish wit. An enlightened, principled man, a Dissenter who seated reason perhaps a bit too near God's throne for some clergy's taste. Overall a man perfectly suited for this new age, this new country and new century soon to dawn. All those qualities the other was alleged to possess must be anticipated in the imaginary dialogues he rehearsed between himself and this powerful white man before he dared present himself at the man's door.

And what of the second voice, his own. Had he neglected proper study of it. What sort of man was he. What gives weight to his words. What does he own, what must *he* protect. Who is he. *Who's there*, this African man hat in hand at the door.

Who's there, please.

Is the woman repeating her question. How long had he stood speechless, lost in the ramble of his thoughts.

He bows deeply. Good day, madam. Beg pardon, madam. By your leave, may I present myself, madam. I am Bishop Allen's messenger. Bishop Allen of Bethel African Church. Dr. Thrush has generously consented to read a petition the bishop and others of his congregation have prepared. I'm here to deliver the said petition and await a reply, if one is forthcoming.

I pray my presence has not discomfited you, madam, and humbly beg your pardon again if it has. This is the hour appointed by Dr. Thrush, but I am truly sorry if I have intruded. I was instructed to wait here by the maidservant who let me in.

I am the intruder, sir. My maid Kathryn on her way to fetch Dr. Thrush informed me we had a visitor. I am the wife of Dr. Thrush. You are welcome in our home, sir.

He would step back, but he is only a step inside the door. Hat a boulder in his hand. Was the letter he'd brought for Thrush still safely nestled in its envelope. First his rambling thoughts, and now a trot of rambling words addressed to this woman, words splashing filth from the gutters on his clothes, spoiling the precious paper entrusted to him. Composure in tatters and he's yet to glimpse the formidable Dr. Thrush. Defending, extenuating, bowing and scraping to what end. Capering before this woman whose arms float at her sides as if no solid floor supports her feet, only some narrow beam upon which she balances.

Are you an African man.

If you please, madam. My mother's mother was transported to these shores from that distant land. But I, good lady, was born south and west of this city, on a farm where my mother too was born.

Are you black, sir.

Yes, madam. And no. To some we Africans are blacks. Others call us coloreds. Some of us once preferred to call ourselves Anglo-Africans. Now I suppose we must be Americans.

But your skin, your color, is it not black.

We are of various hues, madam. Few wear the unadulterated sable shade of our ancestors. Like all the immigrants arriving daily in our great port city, we come from many countries, speak many tongues.

You, sir. What about you. If I may be permitted to ask, what color are you.

I am what you plainly see, madam. What some would designate a brightish mulatto.

I *see* nothing, sir. I am blind, sir. Forgive me please for questioning you so closely. I must borrow other people's eyes since the precious boon of sight was not vouchsafed me. My curiosity leads me to a certain indelicacy of expression and inquiry, I fear. A bluntness others have every right to consider rude.

I'm in your debt, sir, for indulging my questions and manner. Or lack of manners, which indeed may be nearer the case. Thank you. I know you didn't journey here to satisfy my curiosity nor listen to me prattle. Dr. Thrush's study door has just closed behind him. He's on the stairs. He'll arrive in a moment. Good day, sir.

He's heard no door closing, no footfalls, only the rustle of the woman's graceful curtsy. Should he return an invisible bow. He does and she's gone again through a side doorway off the main hall, propelled not as men propel themselves, one heavy leg pushing after the other, but whisked, a gentlewoman's glide, her carriage drawn by a thousand pairs of tiny white mice harnessed and noiseless, concealed beneath her voluminous petticoats.

Hello. Hello, my good man. Dr. Benjamin Thrush, somewhat the worse for wear, at your service. Is it still cold out-of-doors. Yes. You hold a letter for me from Allen, eh. I'll read it immediately and draft my reply. You'll wait, won't you. Please do. Kathryn will fetch you a cup of tea. Below in the kitchen, if you don't mind. Just there, down the steps. Yes. You'll find a comfortable Boston rocker. One of my favorites. Rest yourself. We've all earned it, haven't we. You were one of Allen's worthies, no doubt. Quite a struggle, was it not. I believe I'll need a century of sleep to recover what I lost during the late emergency. Thank goodness for this bracing weather. It cleanses the air. Kathryn will attend you in a moment. I shan't tarry over Allen's epistle. Strange times we live in. A topsy-turvy world, indeed. Yes.

⟡   ⟡   ⟡

Five days blank except for wooden jottings — did this, did that, thus and so still to be done — I've been reminded sternly that neither time nor peace of mind is mine to summon at will — and both are necessary, I find, to this writing affair.

A great commotion boils in the city — now that the worst horrors of the fever seem to have subsided, the town's appetite for scandal has revived full-blown — a letter authorized by a Mr. Mathew Carey attacks the Negroes who served so valiantly during the late calamity — at the height of the emergency Dr. Thrush's letters daily commended the work of black nurses who tended the sick, the black undertakers who removed the dead from the city streets — now Mr. Carey impugns them — accuses the Negroes of charging — nay, extorting — piratous rates for their services — profiting heartlessly from the misery and helplessness of the afflicted.

Carey's bill of particulars against the city's Negroes, alleging blackmail, assaults, robbery, even murder, was recently published as a pamphlet and widely circulated — what's surprising is not that one unhappy soul would conjure up such a distorted picture — who knows how the plague damaged him, who could guess what wrongs, real or imagined, some black person committed against the author or he visited upon a Negro, or what personal grievance became transformed into general enmity toward an entire race — what shocks me is how many citizens, ignoring the evidence of their own eyes and ears, including many who themselves doubtless benefited from the charity and ministrations of the Negro nurses, have embraced Carey's libels as truth.

I blush as I dictate this news, dear Kathryn — a hot flush of shame rises to my cheeks — *as well it should, milady* — it frightens and humbles me that we should have learned so little from our late season of suffering — God warned us, set the plague upon us to demonstrate our unworthiness, our weakness, our dependence on His divine mercy, and what use do we make of the lesson — as soon as danger passes, we turn like cowardly curs on the weak and helpless among us.

Two days ago an emissary from a Bishop Allen of the African Church — the Negroes call themselves sometimes by one name, sometimes by another — I could not pry a preference from our visitor — *why have you never asked my preference* — arrived at our door seeking assistance from Dr. Thrush in this Carey matter — the Negroes believe they are in peril — *yes, yes, yes* — unless leading citizens such as Dr. Thrush step forward and publicly repudiate Carey's charges, the Negroes fear their community, already beleaguered, may be struck a fatal blow — Dr. Thrush summarized to me the contents of their letter — they say the fever hit hardest in those poor, crowded streets and alleys near the river, and that the rate of mortality in that district where most Negroes reside is far higher than anywhere else in the city — people there are starving today, they say, many too ill to work, with little or no work available for the able-bodied, families deprived of wage-earners by the fever's winnowing hand, hapless orphans no cradle but the cold ground — if only half of the Negroes' contentions are true, they have been mightily sinned against — I shudder at the cruel irony — those who suffered most, those who fought hardest to allay its blows, are now being blamed for the plague.

Though he never subscribed to the theory that Negroes from the West Indies brought the plague to our shores, Dr. Thrush himself was part of the chorus insisting upon the Negroes' immunity, thereby denying them assistance until he witnessed with his own eyes how the deadly tide of fever had swept through that neighborhood of hovels, warrens, cellars, of taverns and houses of sin where the poorest folk, Negroes the poorest of these, are trapped.

Now Mr. Carey's libels will imperil them even more — set them apart as pariahs, criminals — in my heart I believe we all, every one of us, must answer one day to our Maker for the un-Christian manner in which we have separated the black folk from ourselves — this latest episode one more instance of a habit so ingrained it has become second nature — I think of my worthy Kathryn — how but for fortune's smile she might be trembling in a cave by the river, helpless, afraid, awaiting the punishment Carey and his rabble are determined to exact.

Your people have a steadfast friend, dear Kate, in Dr. Thrush — you must recall the letter from him you read to me during the last week of September, when the bells mourning the dead tolled from dawn to dusk and hurried missives from my dear husband our sole communication for days at a time — the exacting, soul-wrenching work of saving the city removed all superficial distinctions among men, he wrote — my good husband and his dark angels of mercy welcomed — nay, implored — to attend the highest and lowest citizens — remember how he recounted in his delightful style a conversation with one of his favorite Negro nurses — I can recite his words exactly, an iron memory perhaps one benefit dropped on the scale to balance my lost sight: Huh! Mama. We black folks have come into demand at last.

Always one who judged men on merit, not birth or caste, Dr. Thrush confided to me his profound respect for the skill, patience and compassion he discovered in his black assistants, toiling side by side with them long into the seemingly endless nights — I did not remind him of your example, Kathryn, here in the bosom of his own household — I suspect his silence on your virtues when he waxes eloquent on the potential of the Negro race indicates how completely he regards you as a member of our family, inseparably one of us.

You may rest assured he will speak out for what is right — he will stand beside your people again in their hour of need — *one of us, you say. When there are two, will we still be one of you.*

◇   ◇   ◇

No. No. Do not turn away like some street drudge who's earned her sixpence. Do you think I risk so much simply to enter your bed and thrash about a few moments. No. Please don't twist away. It's not over yet. Not over. Don't turn your back to me. The city is dying. I am a dead man among the dead from morn to night. Though I claim otherwise, for every patient I save, many die. I am cold, cold, awash in the chill of a lie, of black blood and bile. This is the horror I bring to you. Risking both our lives. My bloody hands, my bloody gift. Sink them in the warm silence of your bed. I pray you forgive my icy fingers. Pray for a spark of forgiveness, or pity if you please, even as I take, even as I touch what is forbidden me. Forbidden by God, by law, by your eyes I cannot see, yet hear them screaming no, no. Help me breathe again, make me whole again. Return me to life even as I press breath from you, even as my frozen hands, seeking warmth, pick you apart.

◇   ◇   ◇

Dr. Thrush counsels patience — wounds the fever inflicted upon the city remain raw, he says — now is not the hour for taking sides — let the city heal — we must not foment discord — as a man of science, a voice undeclared, so to speak, he believes he can better serve his black friends by not becoming embroiled in the Carey controversy on one side or the other — act rather as go-between and negotiator, as facilitator of reasonable discourse and compromise — work behind the scenes, reach the ears of all parties — quietly, unobtrusively forwarding the cause of his friends — the general citizens' pain, anger and fear have not subsided, he says — he's sure Carey's pamphlet will excite passions in the mob for a day, then be forgotten — to engage Carey's arguments in public would only draw attention to his clumsy effort, afford his pamphlet the notice, the respectability its author craves — best to let it sink itself — scuttled by the weight of its own sorry prose, sorry logic and lies — no lasting danger in it, Dr. Thrush concludes.

The best men of the city at our door, at our table these last few days — Dr. Thrush's voice has regained some of its former authority among these powerful men — they give no credit to Carey's scurrilous assertions — of course they shan't support Carey — nor shall they oppose him — the most forthright among them admit they must temper their voices, speak softly until public opinion forgives or forgets the fact that many of the best men, including government officials responsible for maintaining the city's welfare, fled the city at the height of the emergency.

Dr. Thrush seconds the counsel of restraint — before all else commerce must be revitalized, the citizens' confidence in their government restored — so many men of substance left the city, chaos has reigned for months — the recovery of the city's health demands an atmosphere of calm and stability — those who would be in charge must ignore the inevitable recriminations, gossip, scandal-mongering that entertain the mob — the best interests of the Negroes lie in a gradual, patient resumption of the natural order of things — a flourishing city will benefit all.

I must admit I am disappointed by these conclusions — sorry Dr. Thrush seems to bend with his peers — perhaps my dear husband is weary — months of fighting the fever have depleted him — perhaps he's recalling the acrimonious debate during the past months when he and his fellow physicians nearly came to blows over competing treatments for the fever — gunpowder cures to blast the air clear of infecting agents, the burning or inhaling of noxious substances, handkerchiefs, scarves, masks, rags soaked in camphor or vinegar, baths hot or cold, sweating, quarantiners who believed the sick and well must be absolutely separated to prevent contamination, a clamor of theories, claims, cures, quacks while the fever raged relentlessly, impervious to all nostrums.

Dr. Thrush, an unwavering advocate of mercury purges and extensive bleeding, broadcast his cure in the newspapers, claiming nearly 100 percent success, if the patient was treated early and rigorously by his method — those who disagreed with him likewise advertised their opinions to the public — Dr. Thrush was attacked on all sides — many old friends turned foe — some went as far as asserting his bleeding of patients already weakened by fever was tantamount to murder — Dr. Thrush was insulted, reviled as a bloody butcher, his practice damaged, his reputation in tatters when the first November frosts mercifully released us from fever's grip.

For a man of honor who values above all else his reputation, yes, if you will, a proud man, even prickly proud on occasion, but a man also whose talents and accomplishments have earned him the esteem, the adulation and respect he's come to accept as his due, for such a man to be called out, challenged, rebuked, scorned in public, was especially intolerable — the rough usage of his person and reputation in the press destroyed his peace of mind — he stormed about the house as if disordered — or sulked — or absented himself for hours in his locked study — I did not recognize in this snappish, brooding person the kind, generous soul who'd won my heart — the servants avoided him — *but he did not avoid one of them* — more than once my own wounded pride sent me scurrying out of his presence after my entreaties, my attempts to help or please, were ignored or, worse, derided and refused.

A most difficult time on all accounts — and frightening — in his prolonged absences I feared the worst — what would become of us — what if he left one morning to tend the sick and never returned, our last hours together spoiled by the bitterness and hurt of that terrible season — I would weep all day — regret my impatience — wonder how much my blindness vexed and incommoded him — ask myself again and again what I might have done better to relieve his suffering mind — why did I only add to his burdens — my useless eyes, useless womb — why did my love prove so paltry — why was it not a bulwark, a safe harbor in his time of need.

His insistence on bleeding his patients — in the newspapers Kate read to me, some called his resolve fanaticism — cost him more than his standing in the medical community — his judgment was questioned — a fellow physician and long-time friend, whose life Dr. Thrush believed he had saved by applications of his purging and bleeding cure, assailed him in the *Gazette* — how many lives, he asked, would the good Dr. Thrush sacrifice before admitting he was wrong.

Perhaps it is a repetition of this vicious campaign of slanders exchanged, of backbiting and name-calling, that Dr. Thrush wishes to avoid — his tireless efforts on behalf of the sick, his decision to remain in the city when so many of his station and calling deserted, were not proof against malicious attacks but have just now begun to reestablish him in the public eye and in the estimation of his peers — thank goodness this fair shift in the weather has also returned to me the confident, spritely, good-natured man I love.

Looking back on those awful days of late summer and fall, perhaps his long absences were a blessing — his work consumed him, distanced him from wicked slander — I learned to miss him desperately — and in the missing rediscover how much there was in him to miss — I swore to myself if given another chance, if normalcy ever returned, I would learn to transform his pained ill humor or, if failing, would endure it without adding the fuel of my unhappiness to the blaze.

All this to say I almost lost him once — if what he lost or feared losing during the time of plague touched him as deeply as I was touched by the prospect of losing him, I can fully understand his reluctance to hazard all once more in this matter of Carey's pamphlet — Dr. Thrush's enthusiasm for the cure he invented cost him dearly — whether his choice of treatment was right or wrong, the agony it occasioned him, us, the chaos of our lives, was for me too great — I would not willingly undergo such a trial again, even to prove him correct — so am I being fair when I feel disappointed about his course of action toward Carey — am I truly willing to link our present happiness, so lately returned, too closely with the fate of a people cursed by God since the trespass of Ham.

No — forgive me, Kathryn — my fellow Christians, not God, fit the yoke of suffering over the necks of our Negro brethren — yes, brethren — what better proof than this Kate in whose hand I place my heart — in her breast beats a heart like mine — her hand in mine, mine in hers the same in God's sight — *poor woman, doubly blind as Carey's shadow falls like an ax between us.*

❖   ❖   ❖

Tonight her dreams are awash in bright colors. She is not blind in her dream but deaf and listening to music. Music become sight not sound. Trumpets and piano trading up-tempo solos. And then she is blind again but remembers the colors of sound and smiles as the silken darkness behind her eyes shimmers, glorious as a rainbow.

❖   ❖   ❖

I must leave you soon, soon you must cure yourself. Can you hear me. Are you listening.

❖   ❖   ❖

How many nights has he come here to sit beside her and tell her stories. How long has he been pretending she's aware of his presence, that what he's saying matters, that give and take, call and response connect them. The others are growing impatient. They see no improvement in her condition. Any visit may be his last. He will knock and no one will answer. He'll know instantly the house is deserted. Even the ghosts gone. He'll panic. Kick down the unlocked door. Burst in out of breath. His whole being crammed into a lump the size of a pea in his throat. He'll see the ladder to the loft broken in pieces on the floor.

Time. He needs more time to cure her. Even to his own ears this plea for more time sounds lame. The voice of a man who's failed. Who's trying to convince himself, convince anybody who will listen, he has not failed. Failed to cure her. Failed to save himself.

If he gets another chance, if they allow him one more visit, this time he'll ask her straightaway what's wrong. Ask why she lies there dying when she has everything to live for. Even if he hasn't been able yet to tell her what these things are. She knows. She must know. If he's allowed one more chance, perhaps she'll hear the word or words she's been waiting for and take up the telling where he must end it.

❖　　❖　　❖

Near the end of his stay on Stubbs' farm, on an unusually warm afternoon, after a morning hacking a few more feet of cultivatable ground from boulders, roots, stones, relentless stubble at one edge of a field, he'd returned early to the barn in order to repair his ax. Sweat-soaked shirt. Skin itching. Forearms streaked with his blood and the blood of insects whose bodies he mashed and bites he scratched.

Sun had been an iron cap nailed to his skull, shrinking tighter and hotter by the minute. The ax's loose handle peeved him, but he welcomed an escape. His back ached, feet burned. He'd started feeling sorry for himself. Always easier when Liam worked beside him. Alone he'd ask too many questions. Am I stuck here forever. Is it time to move on. He'd lose concentration. Work too fast or too slow. Hurt himself. Break things. Fuss at Liam even though Liam wasn't there.

Ox work, old man. Why isn't your scrawny neck locked in the yoke with mine.

Cursing Liam but also grateful Liam had set a task that will exhaust him completely. If he doesn't drop in his tracks at the end of the day and sleep like a dead man under the stars, he'll drag back to the house and sink into a sleep so profound it will shut out the noise of them at each other in the middle of the night. New noises. Night noises he'd come to believe the old couple had lost the knack of conjuring. Nothing all winter. Then spring must have raised the rooster in Liam. Soon, thank Jesus, it would be warm enough to sleep in the barn or sleep outdoors every night.

The sighing and rustle and groan of them a fingertip down his cheek, teasing his eyes open. Then their thrashing a slap in the face startling him wide awake. Awake long after they are snoring again, quiet again, their breathing blended again with the lowing of cattle and sheep, the click and sawing of insects, pop and creak and ache of wood expanding and contracting through its many lives, the raspy whispering of darkness that is a gigantic black river, creeping free of its banks, inching past, the irresistible rub of its black drift changing the shape of everything.

Him wide-eyed, drifting too, in a trance of remembering and forgetting, not quite sure whether he's awake or asleep. Waiting for Liam to free him with the dawn noises of putting the day in order.

Approaching from the west, he slinks into the barn's apron of shadow. Hears Liam. The middle-of-night sound of them making love in the old man's voice.

He doesn't want to spy. No more than he'd ever wanted the light of day to strip the darkness, throw the blanket off the old people grappling in the shadowy pit behind his shoulder. Yet he moves like a hunter, stalking prey in the barn.

Through a chink in the weathered boards he looks past Liam's shoulder to the opposite wall of the barn. She lies there on straw where the cattle sleep. Did she see him, his shadow blotting light from the chink. From the open haying door in the loft, a smoky curtain of light drapes her. Spears of light pierce the barn's roof and walls. She is naked, motionless, propped on an elbow, one leg stretched flat on the straw, the other drawn up at the knee. The noon sun pitiless. Her skin weathered as the wood of the barn.

Liam is painting her. Or painting something he thinks is her, covering a canvas propped on a crude stand with swirls, slurs and spatters of color. He hums and whistles. Liam close enough to touch with the wounded ax if he poked it through this peephole in the wall.

If there is a woman on Liam's canvas, she is beset by a storm of paint. A forest of paint. Flapping pennants of paint. Triangles and rectangles. Colors he'd never seen before, mashed, streaked, spattered, running like yolk from broken eggs. Feathers of paint. Ladders. Ropes. Dark fists inside the paint pounding to get out. Somewhere in the holler of it, the woman's figure surely was forming, surely as patches of familiar melody formed the quilt of Liam's tune.

When he looks at her again, beyond the canvas, through it, she's changed. Transformed as air and water and fire had turned her into different women, many women crowding the room that first morning when he had watched her bathe in the split cask beside the fireplace.

Not the woman stretched on this burning straw, not the woman twisting free of rainbowed serpents of paint. Not what Liam imagined or he imagined or she imagined, but what could come next. After this time. Next and next. Always unknown. Always free.

◇　　◇　　◇

Why do I write "Dr. Thrush" — is this man who strides so regally through the pages of my little book not my Benjamin — my dear Ben, my B — I admit to a sort of little-girl silly stammering when he appears here and I must choose to call him something — Him, He, My husband, Master, Love — why do I tag him with the oh-so-formal "Dr. Thrush" — is he such an august personage that nothing less than a title does him justice — what would he name me in his book — is the solemn "Dr. Thrush" a shield I advance to protect him — or protect myself — to cover my excitement as I picture him, his handsome countenance and noble, manly form — do I fear tripping over my own feet in a wanton dash to embrace him — memories of shared secrets and passion a blush spreading from my toes to the crown of my head — must I restrain myself — remind myself he is also one I must share with the world — endeavor, therefore, always to honor him as the world understands a wife's duty — my fine, accomplished, esteemed, good Dr. Thrush — would I be undressing him in public by calling him anything less than Dr. Thrush.

Henceforth, you shall be B — naked or not — when you enter these pages — I pray I do not discomfit you by this shortness of address — I pray sweet Kate's modesty is not offended as you traipse through my thoughts in high deshabille — and you, darling husband, do not be offended by this stripping away of your title — consider it a labor-saving measure so Kate's hand may fly Ariel-like that much more swiftly upon its errands.

❖   ❖   ❖

B- B-B-B — I'm being read a novel of Samuel Richardson's in which there appears a Mr. B — though a handsome B, as you are, he possesses few of your virtues, and fortunately, you none of his loathsome vices — but you are both B's — it is the fashion in certain scandalous novels to conceal the identity of characters taken from life by employing initials in place of names — of course this conceit — borrowed from the French, I believe, their notorious "roman à clef" — whets rather than curbs appetite for scandal — titillating as much as concealing, because the adventures narrated in the fiction are by this conceit of initials also insinuated to be real — real enough to incriminate someone — if not incriminating, if not real, why the cloak of initials — the reader may have his — or her, since I'm told most readers of novels are of the idle feminine tribe — cake and eat it too — gentle readers invited to spy on the intimate doings of their betters and also permitted to disclaim any immoral or prurient interest in such spying, since after all, what's being read is mere make-believe, a novel, is it not — I pity the lords and ladies, people of quality, the notable or star-crossed citizens whose bones are picked by our modern authors — their lives laid bare before the public's eye with only the fig leaf of an initial to cover their modesty.

Rest easy, sir — I promise not to use you thusly — sell your secrets, dear B, for sixpence — I shall be the only reader of these scribblings — I have no wish to pen a novel — besides, no fanciful prince I could contrive would be as brave and handsome, more silly and lovable than thou, my actual B, I draw exactly from life.

While I'm in this literary vein — I must reveal a secret I've been bursting to tell — I purchased your birthday gift and am mightily pleased by it — a book I wish to thrust instantly into your hands — but since your birthday is still a month away I must act the part of a patient adult — keep your gift hidden till the appropriate moment — I can hardly bear it — this restraint when I am as you know so well all gush and giggle and blurt when it comes to keeping pleasant secrets.

Ahh . . . I feel better now — my secret's out — though it shall go no further than these secret pages.

Do you recall the African girl Phillis, said to be the first of her race to publish a book of poems — much controversy surrounded the appearance of her little book of verse — many said she could not possibly have learned, in the short time she'd been here, the English language well enough to write verse — others argued her tender age itself barrier enough to prevent her being authoress of poems the best of which have been favorably compared with the productions of Mr. Pope — so great was the general disbelief her Boston publisher convened a panel of distinguished scholars and esteemed men of affairs to examine the girl — she passed with flying colors — book and authoress, I'm told, enjoyed a season of celebrity — though not as fashionable today, it remains a touching, elegant book, if I am any judge of such matters — I can't wait to hear you pronounce upon it — and hear you read — though Kathryn has ably rendered the poems to me in her melodious voice, from your lips they will be born anew.

I hope the book will delight you — the range of subjects is surprising in one so young, so new to craft and country both — a testament to the genius of the despised African race — one more proof of the rightness, the fitness of your long crusade on behalf of these unfortunate, misunderstood, abused children of God.

The book, the African girl who composed it, bring to mind our Kate — so wise, observant, gentle and compassionate — I've encouraged her to try her hand at setting down her thoughts — yet I fear she may be too wearied by the tedious labor of recording mine — even as I tendered my suggestion I realized how much she's at my side, how much I demand of her — how she is always at the ready, anticipating my needs before I know what they are myself — who knows what eloquence she might achieve, freed from the constant round of her duties — so full of feeling — *full of his ravenous seed that hollows out a place within me, devouring me from inside — as you from outside — digging, scooping.*

❖   ❖   ❖

The boy shivers. Cold never leaves him. He stares through parchment faces of the men examining him. Remembers the watchman's tale.

In that faraway country across the sea we were giants, the watchman had lied to him. Every one these fingers long as a man. Dark hand thrust in the boy's face. A goblin's claw.

Then white ants come. Put us sleep. Taken us apart bone by bone. Boil giant bones in kettle ships till them bones tiny as these here you see now in my crooked hand. Little-bitty like they white ant bones. Break big bones, boil dem down. Den puts us back togedder again.

White ants make powerful juju. But magic good for make men sleep, magic good for shrink bone and break bone, not good magic for put bones back togedder. Bone no fit. Ache and ache. Cold and dark in dere where bone not tight. Not nice and tight and strong like dem big bone.

In the cellar where he was locked every night wind moaned through those empty spaces the watchman's words had named. The cellar's cold floor a desert of bones. Whispering rat feet scurry across the sand. Never quiet in the joints and crevices of his body. *Will these bones live again. Rise again.* He'd hear the other children stirring, busy with their night visitors. One coughs, another whines, one snorts, one weeps, noise all night inside his ear whether he's awake or asleep, the tidings of the cellar plying through him, inescapable whether his eyes open or shut.

He dreams of sickly little Abraham on his straw pallet, face like a chewed apple the morning after he had died during the night, died too weak to cry out or bat away the rats feasting on his cheeks.

You are the lucky ones, they said. Mothers and fathers gone to God, they said. The terrible fever took them, but merciful God spared you. God your father and mother now, and unto Him you must render all praise and devotion. In this shelter erected in His name you must make yourselves worthy of God's blessing. You must learn to serve Him faithfully every moment of every day His goodness grants you on this earth.

Deponent sayeth:

We sleep in a cellar. Below rooms where they feed us and teach us. On the top floor, above the rooms where we spend our days, are rooms where angels live. Closer to Heaven. In rooms warm and clean. Where they take us to do God's work, scouring every inch of the top floor so it is spotless and the bright faces of the angels shine back at them from the surfaces we scrub and polish, doing God's work.

We are many colors, children of many colors, but the cellar turns us all black. I cannot see my own hands and my hands cannot see my black face in the darkness of the cellar. I am one and many down there. Where I end and another begins is never clear. No one can be sure. I suck another's thumb. Someone uses my asshole to break wind. On the coldest nights we clump together for warmth and our hearts beat as one, we shiver as one, we cough and spit and wet and the pile rolls to crush or expel what it cannot abide.

Like the dead we listen for our names in the dark. Our hands cannot tell us who we are or who we are not. If we dare call out the names of our mothers and fathers, it will bring, as our singing or moaning brings, pounding on the floor above our heads. The watchman sleeps in his chair beside the cellar door. If we persist in disturbing him, we hear the creaking gate lift, his heavy steps down the ladder, the rungs squealing as he descends. *Hush, hush, hush, hush* a lullaby he grunts with each lash of the strap.

Once the watchman told me I would die if I ever fell asleep stretched out full length on the floor. He said that's why he sleeps upright in his chair. To trick death. For weeks I sat or dreamed I sat up to keep off death, propping myself against anyone who would not shove me away.

I am one of the rulers here. Large enough to hurt the others so I am feared. I am a thief. We are slopped with meager scraps from the tables of the top floor. To survive I steal food from the weak and foolish. I choose my victims carefully. We become partners in a long, slow dance of starvation. My crimes an amusement for the others. They cheer my ruthlessness, tease my victim, mock the tottering, dazed frailty.

There is art as well as policy in my practice. Leaving a tithe to keep breath in the starving one, reaping enough to maintain my advantage, keep the others at bay. I take no pleasure in prolonging the misery of my victims, yet each must suffer long enough to lull the rest into believing I won't ever need to turn on one of them.

◇　　◇　　◇

Dearest B — this morning, though you have long ago departed for your duties, I feel a pressing desire to speak to you — so I shall — speak as I do in my prayers — speak to you as I address this little book — speaking to it as I have always yearned to speak to you.

I share secrets with my book — it's already an old, treasured friend — I ask it questions about myself and the marvel is, sometimes it answers — yesterday, for instance, I inquired: why do I write — without hesitation it replied: because you are lonely — well, I blushed of course and apologized to my numerous dear friends and acquaintances, to Kathryn beside me as always setting down the silliness that sneaks from my lips, my heart — apologized for the book's impertinence most of all to you, kind, indulgent B — I could not, however, deny the truth of the book's reply — yes, I am lonely, yes, in spite of those who care for me — yes — I write because there is always too much to say or nothing to say — no words to speak to another — no words another would understand — even if someone was willing or able to listen.

But here you are before me now — I conjure your presence

with each word I address to you — I imagine the arch of your brow when I pique your curiosity or say something outrageous and you're not quite sure whether you heard me correctly or you heard me all too well — I can almost see your gentle frown or teasing smile.

My days at the shelter are long and hard — now that I am gone so much from our home, we see even less of one another than before — those precious moments together that passed too, too swiftly seem now, from this distance, like sumptuous oases of time — when all we had were those brief moments, I fussed, wanting more — dreamed, then wished aloud (selfishly and too often, I fear) for a change in our pattern of living — little did I know change was on its way, but a change that would allow us less, not more, time together.

I am consumed by my orphans — I thank you daily, though you seldom hear me express my gratitude since it flows at times like this when I can't squeeze your hand nor feel the warmth of your gaze, times when I am full of unspoken thank-yous for raising the funds that established a shelter and school, for encouraging me to become part of the enterprise — Thank you, thank you, because I depend on your loving counsel and support when the whole world seems to be caving in upon me and my destitute charges.

You must visit us soon — the school, the orphan children, have become a new family for me — I'm afraid I shamelessly mother them as much as teach them — they yearn to meet their papa — I've told them all about you — how without your efforts no shelter would exist — they know you well from a distance and from that distance love you already — but I am teaching them to be greedy for more of you, their benefactor and protector — as I am greedy for you — summoning you here to stand at attention before my desk like one of my small pupils.

Do not tremble, sweet boy — my lecture is nearly over — a painless lesson — my sole, uncharitable impulse to remind you of the burden of my love — put more plainly, I miss you dreadfully — yet at this hour I can no more cut back on my time at the school than you can shorten the hours required to treat your patients, rebuild the town — we must content ourselves with the knowledge that the same divine, guiding spirit that places you at the center of the struggle to mend our broken city has given me a role to play at the margin — where, in spite of my blindness, my modest talents, I find need and welcome among the Negro orphans.

I think I may have begun this entry to complain, perhaps scold you for being so much away — instead I'm confessing how busy, how much away, I too have been — yet I must gratefully thank Providence for assigning the duties lately keeping us apart.

Complaint, scolding or confession — it matters little what I call things here, since no one, not even you, B, will see my book — in its pages I am accountable to no one but myself — nor do I hold myself strictly accountable to myself — certainly not to the woman who considers herself rational, logical, endowed with at least a sprinkling of female decorum and reserve.

One last word — or warning, if you will — when we find more time to spend together, do not be surprised if at first you do not recognize your devoted mate — I embarked on a mission to save other souls — but I discover they are saving mine — and in the process I sense myself changing — molting, growing new feathers.

Kathryn tells me my new plumage is becoming — she says I

glow when I work with the children — Kathryn as usual spoiling me — she delights in making more of me than I am — and though I worry I am too much indulged by my loyal maidservant, I anxiously await the opportunity of being spoiled even more lavishly, as only you, my B, spoil me.

◇　　◇　　◇

Deponent sayeth further:

Yes, I remember the first day I saw the women here, the pale one and the one my color who was the other's shadow, her eyes. I hated both of them immediately, their flouncing gowns, their fluttering voices breaking the silence of winter rooms. The black one. The blind one who would never find me unless the dark scout led her to my hiding places. I despised their soft, unmarked hands. Their ease and flow entering this place they know they can leave whenever they choose. Pretending to be something they are not, pretending we who live here are something we are not. They forget the flesh and blood beneath their airs and their finery, forget they are women just as surely as I'll be a man someday whether dressed in rags or king's robes, a man the day I rip the clothes off their bodies and stuff my truth between their legs.

The Bible teaches us, the white one said, and then the words she recited were fingers kneading the back of my neck, ungentle fingers squeezing, pulling, as if to awaken me and put me to sleep at the same time. Fingers pulling me apart and patting the torn flesh into soft patties dead as sausage.

They come — the blind one who sees nothing, the dark one who sees everything but the color that makes her one of us. They come to teach us. They are our teachers. I asked the watchman, what is a teacher. He stares at me, grizzled wolf at rabbit he's wounded and cornered. The foul pipe as always in his mouth. Most days he can't beg tobacco and the pipe hangs unlit from his fat lips. He puffs and sucks anyway, a dirge of crackling in the stem. He pulls the pipe from his mouth. Spit, not ash, when he taps the upended bowl.

Teachers are the dead, he says. Come teach you pikken how to die. The heavy lids of his eyes drop. The watchman doesn't need to fix me in his stare any longer. Bloody tendons dangle from the rabbit's twitching legs. He forgets me. His head droops, he's nodding, gone wherever the dead rule, listening to them teach.

Sometimes when the watchman answers me, his answers like dogs suddenly unleashed, unpenned, dashing off in galloping circles everywhere at once. Answers not ending when I return to my chores. The watchman's mumbling, his language I barely understand, plagues my ear for the rest of the day. Most often he ignores my questions. Shoos me. Hits or kicks if I stray too close. Once he spit on me. Spraying my bare toes with a gush of tobacco juice the color of blood.

For hours he sits, blind, deaf and dumb, with the pipe clenched in his jaw, rocking back and forth, asleep with his eyes wide open. In the silence he questions me. Ghost of his voice whining inside my ear. *Who are you. Why are you here. Where do you belong.*

When he rocks up and back, up and back, his body on the stub-legged stool, wagging like a tongue, I can touch him. I'm sure he doesn't feel my hands on his tarry skin. On his prickly chin. I finger the furrows of his brow, the creases in his cheeks deep as folds of the shambling turban twisted round his head.

I have touched the pipe when it's hot. When it's cold. He plays it, a piper summoning invisible flocks, rocking up and back, up and back, floating in a kind of sleep.

The watchman knows the women don't belong here. Why don't they understand we are stuffed in this shelter to die. If the women wish to teach us, they should come at night, to the cellar. Teach us down there. Teach the dead, let the dead teach them. Teach the dark one her color. Teach a blacker darkness to the one with no eyes. Let us teach them with our hands and tongues and toes. In the cellar there is no scrambling away from the one next to you who touches you where you think you don't want to be touched. You understand that the fingers trespassing are your fingers, the stink yours, the wetness yours. You learn that morning, if it ever dawns, changes nothing. Though you mount the ladder from cellar to other floors, the light you yearned for all night in the cellar's darkness does not free you. Its chore when it blazes is to separate you from the others so you can each climb the ladder, go about your duties, receive the punishments due you, the lessons, cleaning other people's filth, the hateful slop you steal and gobble so you don't starve. The light changes none of it.

At first I thought the dark one merely the pale one's shadow, mincing behind her, echo, reflection, toy dog on invisible chain. Then I noticed from my seat in the rear of the room how the white one falters, her smile tightens, how her hands paddle in the air like a drowning man's when the other strays too far from her side. I can almost hear her praying for sight, praying for the cushion of air the other's arm provides, praying for the other woman whose color she cannot see is my color.

I want to laugh out loud at them. Run to the blind one and shove my arm into the emptiness her pale fingers ply. Let her find me, teach her my strength, my color, let her lean on my arm, then jerk it away.

She learns quickly. Too quickly she becomes sure of herself, her dead eyes roaming free in this place where after many months I still bump into things and stumble and grope and fear for my life every moment of every day and night. She quickly learns the syllables of our names and speaks them precisely to us . . . Isaiah Cudjo Elizabeth Phyllis Hannibal Chloe Thomas Mary Jupiter Grace Sarah . . .

Calls each of us perfectly by the syllables of our names to answer her questions, as if the names belong to her, not us, as if our dead mothers and fathers, brothers and sisters do not rush into the room, howling and moaning, snatching back our names.

God sent the fever to purge us. To cleanse. To humble us, the blind one said. We who have survived must struggle to build a new city. A better city. The plague orphaned you but it has spared you also. No one can replace your lost loved ones, but you are not alone, children. God has granted you an opportunity to prepare yourselves in this school for the long, hard journey ahead. Your parents are gone, but a kind God has not deserted you. Before we begin the lesson, let us bow our heads and pray for strength and guidance.

Our Father who art . . .

in this heaven heaven heaven

Heaven of her perfume, the flounce of her blue sleeves, her gown's blue whisper. What kind god has spent hours wrapping this sweet-smelling gift taller than I am so I may sniff it and peek at it but not open.

A.

A for able. A for angel.

A, children. Repeat after me. A for able. A for angel.

He is a quiet one, Kathryn. A shy one.

They both touch me. White hand. Black hand. One my shoulder. One pats my head. My skin burns and puckers. Streamers of flesh stripped from the crown of my skull, a searing hot iron brands me down to the bone, shivering dreadlocks of flesh drape my back.

Oh. He shrinks from my touch. I'm so sorry. Excuse me, child. Please excuse me. I am too free with my hands. Forgive me. My hands are my eyes. I did not mean to frighten you.

Come. Come, sir. You will survive this awful assault. Wipe the frown from your face. We are not cannibals. Come now, young man. A for able. A for angel.

Do I detect a hiss at least. If a whisper the most you can manage today, thank you for your whisper, sir. But louder next time. Loud and clear with the others.

His chest heaves. A crackling in his throat like the watchman's gurgling pipe. The blind one can't see him. If he gouges out his own eyes, will the women disappear. He squeezes his eyes shut against them, presses his lips together and breathes through his nose. His nostrils flare. Eyes water. He will explode unless he tames what's rising inside him, swelling his heart in his chest, constricting his throat. He wants to leap off the bench and knock them down. The white one first, then her shadow. Stomp them both. The black one second because he knows once he starts in on her, he won't be able to stop.

*

The Cattle Killing ◇ 195

The examiners nod. White chins sink into black robes, eyes close. A wish for music plays in his head. Music he's never heard before, or heard once and forgotten till this moment, or music no one has invented yet. Music he could use to bundle his rage and wrestle it to the ground the way he'd seen men with blankets and burlap sacks grab burning people as they fled from an inferno engulfing a row of shanties along the riverfront. Some fool had set the blaze, exploding gunpowder to cleanse the air of fever. People would believe that lie. He'd say yes, yes, it happened that way.

Music to restore a sane rhythm to his breathing. Music to free the children. Music of human torches, scrawny, crooked little legs running in circles. The crowd screaming, men with blankets throwing them over the children's heads. Tiny hooded shadows dropping to the ground.

Music for plucking the pipe from the sleeping watchman's mouth, music for creeping down the ladder into the pitch-black cellar, the red glow of the bowl bobbing rung by rung as he descends, the pipe's terrible taste as he sucks it to keep it burning, a shower of sparks shaken onto the straw heaped at the ladder's foot. Quickly up again. Door creaking as he eases it shut. Both feet holding it down as he slides the latchboard in place. Flames already crackling below. The watchman nodding on his stool, great puffs of smoke rising from the empty pipe that dangles again from his lips.

Music of the watchman's steady drift up and back, rocking on his stool. Music with no name. For free children. For children cooked alive. For the cellar's darkness. A simple, cleansing music to slow his breathing, loosen the hand gripping his throat. Music for the cloud of her intoxicating perfume thick in the air above his head.

Music prophesying the fury of the beating he'll earn when he grabs her and sinks his teeth in her throat. Black teeth into the white throat of one. White teeth into the black throat of the other.

Guilty.

Guilty.

Guilty.

Guilty, the pillar of each face intones.

May God have mercy on your soul.

◇   ◇   ◇

Kathryn, my Kate — you tremble — your tears strike the page — pray tell me, dear girl — please tell me what's wrong.

Now the trembling, the tears are mine — Kathryn's hand steady now, as I implored her to be — we must not stop now — the pen scratches while I speak — yet I never hear it then — hear it only when I am silent, listening for it to catch up so I may begin again — myself real on the page, alive only when I'm composing my story, unaware of myself, real until I hear the pen and then there is only waiting, the silence when it stops.

Every day you sit at the desk and write — yet you are a blur — a scent, the scratching of a pen, your gown's rustle, a gown if I ask you might say is blue today — blue, as if blue can be said — you are a voice reining me in if I speak too fast — a sigh when your generous heart shares some woe of mine I ask you to record — yet this blue, these fragments, are what I possess to remind me daily who you are — the inconsequence of who I am to you — moving as I do, as you do, as we all must, through the margins of someone else's world — a mere passing presence in another's story — unless someone decides to make more of you, account for you in some manner or other, draw you into the space where he sits, imaginary king on imaginary throne, imagining a fate for you in his palace, his kingdom and country that are nothing more than passing presences in the margin of someone else's dreamy tale.

No. Kathryn does not tremble now — she is not crying — I cannot pretend she is the reason my words are shaking — even if I possessed eyes this morning, eyes alive and clear as hers, I could not hold a pen, steer it across a page.

We share a secret now — a secret neither of us has said the words of — we are not ready to say them, though we both know we must — words shaming us, so unsaid — words locking us into an unholy, silent pact — we say only what we need to say to preserve the silence — words stillborn — no words for the roundness of belly she grasped my hand and forced me to feel — no name for the touchable shape, nor name for the untouchable shape inside it — no name we can say now — wounded doubly by silence — the pain of it stretched between us — the pain of not having attempted to break the silence — until now — until the pen is unmoving on the page and there is only waiting, no words for telling more.

❖ ❖ ❖

He closes the blind woman's book. The book entrusted to him he opened and searched for clues only after he'd lost her again. Considers for the first time in a very long while a prayer. Not for the lost ones in the pages of this book he is reading. No, they are long gone, strangely antique in their gowns and knee breeches and stockings and chains. No. It was the endless parade of grieving, afflicted, injured souls like those in the book that had finally stopped his prayers in his throat. He could cry over them no longer, pray over them no more without forfeiting his own will to live.

The prayer he considered an instant, before it too seemed futile, a prayer for souls already irretrievably lost, lost, lost, the prayer he believed for a moment he might utter, was a prayer for the unborn, the unimagined.

A prayer of thanksgiving. If the new ones somehow manage to arrive, he needs to thank them. A wordless prayer of thanksgiving passing from here to there. A prayer not to any god anyone has named. A prayer thanking the ones still buried in the folds of this tainted beginning. This fallen place. Amen.

A terrible thought: the prayer might boomerang and fling him back to his own beginning and he would have to kneel there and open his mother's legs and see himself curled asleep, see everything in a blast of white light that also shouts *no no no* because surely as the light reveals it also separates. The seed of him shrivels. His mother moans. Both of them shot and tossed in a ditch beside the road.

◈   ◈   ◈

The dead say the children are asleep in the cellar. They starve there. They are tortured there. They freeze. Sicken. Are eaten by insects and vermin. They are deprived of sunlight and loving touch and the nurturing light of the best others have spoken and written. Even if they survive, they are blighted forever by the cellar. And worst of all, they have been orphaned — have only the dead to care for them, care about them. We have lost them and they have lost us and that is why we are the dead.

⟡   ⟡   ⟡

They'd meet on Sundays. His preaching days over. Sunday mornings free for him now. Her family off to the white church, disappointed she does not accompany them, but understanding, appreciating her reluctance to attend services there, even if the deacons could be convinced that her special role in the family as a blind woman's eyes should exempt her from sitting in the gallery with the other colored worshipers. Thus she was permitted to attend the African church. But instead, each Sunday morning she walks past Allen's church, past the hulking Quaker jail to the foot of Walnut, turns left on Water Street, negotiates a maze of nameless alleys and byways to his room above the Hart and Hare.

Since the day they met in the hallway, both disconcerted by encountering an unknown person of color in a white man's house, a place accessible only with the white man's permission, both embarrassed by the ritual of undressing, sounding out one another — *whose Negro is this and how has this Negro been treated by the whites who own it and does it speak for them, like them, has it been broken, tamed by them, should I pity it or despise it or cringe from its pain and its shame or put it in its place, one-up its airs with mine. Will I see nothing or see my own face in the mirror of this other whose eyes search mine for confirmation or dismissal or love. What have they done to you, baby. Sweet Jesus, what have they done . . .*

— since that day they met in the walnut-paneled, parquet-floored hall, met in the hallway, met, met, met, they've stolen Sunday mornings. Sunday morning the only time the Hart and Hare sleeps. Spent the morning together in the peace and quiet of his cupboard-sized room, on the shelf of his bed that is like a berth on a ship whose close wooden walls smelling of tar and a thousand cargoes enclose them, the hide of a vessel they journey in as far as the ends of the earth.

Let me take your hand. Please. It's all right. Cry. Cry if you need to cry.

He comes for me in the middle of the night, when she is sleeping. As if the darkness of night is a cover for his wicked trespass. For his betrayal of her. For the hurt and humiliation he inflicts on me. As if darkness could conceal anything from her, poor soul doomed to live in perpetual night. As if she has not taught herself to weave a kind of seeing from the dark, a mysterious acuity compensating for her useless eyes. It's more than a heightening of her remaining senses. She dreams a world around herself, an animated painting she is able to slip into, where she can move with ease and familiarity, though to other eyes her painting is nothing but emptiness framed, a black pit, a void.

Because I am so much in her company, my faculties have sharpened in a vain attempt to match hers. I believe I can hear with her sharp ears how he steals from their marriage bed, creeps through the house to my cot, hear him settle into it, making himself master of it and of me. I think I hear the anguish of her stillness, stillness so much like mine, lying in her bed pretending to sleep while the messages of what he's doing wash over her, messages that become kicks and screams and fists smashing into us both. What to others would be the barely perceptible prattle of night is a storm to her, a storm whose destructive course she plots inch by inch as it tears her world apart.

I feel her trapped inside me, looking out at him. She is inside him too. Looking down on me. His face looming over me, his wet mouth devouring a body he can't see. Him shrouded by the absolute, windowless darkness of my tiny maid's chamber, but she can discern his shape against larger, deeper shadows, detaching itself, hovering, then sinking, his heavy head a blackened sun dropping below the horizon of my shoulder to my bosom.

Rasp of his hand across my bare skin — shameless blending of his stinks and mine — water sloshing in a pail — bones cracking — eely loins slapping together — pump of his bellows chest — choked-off gasps deep in my throat I must swallow — *ah ah ah* — before they become screams that would wake the whole household.

Five feet away, on the other side of my door, you'd suspect nothing — but if you are the woman at the far end of the house, pretending sleep but wide-wide awake, you miss nothing of the racket — though I muffle my sighs and groans — though in spite of his pinches and jerks and bites and squeezes I lie as frozen as she is — though I still my tongue, chew my lip till blood mixes in my spit, she hears the red seeping — hears his mouth smacking when he pries my lips open to taste the salty gruel.

You must do something to stop him. Let me . . .

Do, do, do. *Do*, you say. What can anyone do now. Would you kill him. And when they hunt you down, I'm left with your blood on my hands. Too much done already. The deed's done already and nothing now for me but waiting. For truth to swell my belly. For truth to out.

But I want to help you.

You've helped enough already. Inviting me here. Listening. Treating me with respect and kindness, as you would a friend. Sharing your stories. I look forward all week to these meetings. They save me. I only wish I'd found you sooner. Or you had found me. I imagine different lives for us. What we might have been if we'd spent a life together.

Sometimes I wonder if anything I say reaches you. Why should it. How could it. I fear . . .

As if she has heard the rest of his thought and there is no need for him to say it aloud, she interrupts him with a smile. Like the walls of St. Matthew's that day she appeared, the walls of his room above the Hart and Hare collapse. The entire world begins to slip into their secret space. But as the crowd grows larger and larger, the space easily accommodates them all, becomes more secret, more private.

I finally confessed to Bishop Allen that I'd lost my faith. Told him I must leave the church. Preach no more. Just before the memorial service at the orphanage. It seemed the worst time to tell him. The best also. I was angry at him. I think I wanted to hurt him. I couldn't imagine how he could compose himself to address the crowd gathering to mourn the children. Your children. It was the god he presumed to serve whose kindness had spared the children from the fever, orphaned them, set them apart in a shelter, allowed that shelter to burn to the ground with the children trapped inside. How could Allen face the people, how could he speak as emissary of such a god.

I knew my small defection meant nothing in the face of the terrible loss of the children's lives. Yet I chose to add my paltry news to Allen's burdens that morning. Yes. I endeavored to hurt him. Break him. Add my straw. I hoped it might be one straw too many, that he might falter, turn away from a god who authors an endless chain of horrors for African people.

Allen is a great man. A large-souled man. He listened. Did not utter a word in response. Then he touched my forehead. Smiled. Or rather he looked at me in a certain way I thought of as a smile for want of a better word, the way you might say the sky smiled or a river smiled in a story you make up.

I can hurt him, I did hurt him, I believe. But the hurt, all the hurt in the world, would not stop him. So like my dear lost mother. The good bishop's capacity for pain, for bearing pain others cannot bear, is endless. I guess I knew I could depend on his strength even as I opened my mouth to add selfishly, spitefully, a bit more pain that morning before he left his church to address the mourners.

From this blackened pit, from the precious ashes of these little ones called to Jesus' side, the hopes of our people will rise again . . .

Yes. He dared say those words. Believed them. And the ashes of my faith were mixed with the children's bones and blood and stilled laughter, and if Allen's words meant anything, if anyone anywhere listened to his sermon, perhaps my doubt was sea-changed, rose too.

You were there. You heard him. He preached a magnificent sermon. And when it was over the silence descended on us, didn't it, like one of those sudden snowstorms in the fall. The first snowstorm of the season falling from a blue, windless sky. Huge flakes hovering in the air. One by one changing everything. It takes your breath away, so beautiful and strong and irresistible you don't want it ever to end, but it frightens you also because you understand very well it may not end, does not have to stop. One day the snow, the silence, won't stop. They will cover you, smother you, end you. And perhaps this is the very day. This could be the d-d-d-day.

Then the way one of them always does, some old sister lines out a verse and everybody joins in. The singing starts up not to break the silence, but to enter the deep river of it and s-s-s-swim after the children.

As you hear, I've begun to stutter. Even when I'm not speaking. Stuttering. Losing my facility in this language that's cost me far too much to learn. Cost too much of this life and countless other lives. A stutter. Between what I want to say and the saying of it, a shadow passes. A ditch opens and the words crumple and drop into it. Fly away, fly away home, my words a face in the mirror I do not want to recognize.

Time now to give it up. This speaking in a strange tongue, this stranger's voice I struggle to assume in order to keep you alive. The stories are not working. I talk, maybe you listen, but you're not better, not stronger. I'll lose you any minute. You cannot live in this fallen place. Love can't live here. Time to go. Give it up. Let you go and go with you. Wherever. Across the sea, the stars, as far as you'll let me.

I'm sta-sta-starting to sta-sta-sta-sta-stutter.

The language coming apart in my hands. The way the blue gown shredded when you knelt in the sand beside the lake and pulled the tired cloth over the child's golden crown of curls.

She studies him. She's not sure whether he's playing a game or words are truly sticking in his throat. A silly make-believe to turn back disaster or some awful malady affecting him.

Either way, something is terribly wrong and he can't do a thing, she can't do a thing to change it, so she says, No matter, no matter, it's fine, baby. You're fine. Letting him know she understands and it's all right. Either way. Everything. Any way. As long as you tried your best, baby. Fine. Fine. Fine.

◇   ◇   ◇

One day when it's time to tell the last story and I stutter because it sits like a stone in my throat and carries the weight of all the stories told and untold I wanted to bring you as gifts, stories of my dead to keep you alive, to keep love alive, to keep me coming here each evening to be with you in spite of my dead, in spite of what was missing, lost, unaccounted for, never to be found again, in spite of the earth turning faster underneath us so each time I walk through your door there is less time and more time to be mourned, to be mounted in the stories I hoped would bind us, free us so always there would be more, more . . .

One day I will tell you about Ramona Africa in her cell and Mandela in his cell and the names of the dead we lit candles for in Philadelphia, in Capetown, in Pittsburgh. Here. Take my blind hand. Teach it your features. Forgive me my dead. Loosen their grip on my heart. I breathe through their stories. If I ever kiss you, it will be with lips that form them. My dead in the kiss. The crowd that never showed up the afternoon of the rally in Philadelphia's Independence Square to mourn the dead of Osage Avenue. Half a million people thronging the square in Capetown, spilling onto surrounding streets, like Hitchcock's birds lining every bridge, embankment, highway overpass and road, black and white at the rally welcoming Mandela back after twenty-seven years in prison.

I must warn you there are always machines hovering in the air, giant insects with the power to swoop down spattering death, clean out the square in a matter of instants. All our flesh, millions of arms and legs, powerless, bodies crushed, trampled, ripped apart by a rain of fire from machines driven by men not unlike the ones sprawled below in the square, the dead left behind by the multitude the machines have stampeded away.

And warn you there are prophecies in the air, prophecies deadlier than machines. If you deny yourselves, transform yourselves, destroy yourselves, the prophets say, a better world will be born. Your enemies will be dismayed, disarmed by your sacrifice, and be your enemies no more. From the ashes of your sacrifice a new world of peace and plenty will arise, they say. The prophets of ghost dance, prophets of the cattle killing, prophets of Kool-Aid, prophets of bend over and take it in your ear, your behind, prophets of off with your head, prophets of chains and prisons and love thy neighbor if and only if he's you, prophets of one skin more equal than others and if the skin fits, wear it and if it doesn't, strip it layer by layer down to the bone and then the prophets sayeth a new and better day will dawn.

Pittsburgh and Chicago and Los Angeles and Detroit and New York and Dallas and Cleveland and Oakland and Miami, up and down the land in all the cities, there are funerals and rallies and each is a story, a celebration and mourning and letting go and gathering, different stories over and over again that are one story. Death keeping someone alive, till another day, another story. Ramona lights her candle — passes it to Mandela — passes it to Mumia — passes it to Huey — passes it to Goodman and Chaney — passes it to Gabriel — passes it to the ghost of a woman finding herself, naming herself at one of the rallies in one of the cities where I search for you, to join you, save you, save myself, tell you stories so my dead are not strangers, so they walk and talk, so they will know us and welcome us. Free us. To love.

Tell me, finally, what is a man. What is a woman. Aren't we lovers first, spirits sharing an uncharted space, a space our stories tell, a space chanted, written upon again and again, yet one story never quite erased by the next, each story saving the space, saving itself, saving us. If someone is listening.

EPILOGUE

Dan had laid aside the outline, the notes for his book on the slave castle at Goree, and finished his father's book during the final leg of the long plane ride over from the States. If the clouds would ever disperse, the green motherland should soon appear below.

Tea, sir. Hot tea. Here you are, sir.

An engaging, intriguing book, as most of his father's books were for him. And as most of his father's books, this one also seemed inspired by something unsaid, unshared, hidden. Silent at the core. Stuff maybe his father couldn't say. Full of silence and pain at the core. The same shit they could never get to, let alone deal with when they talked. What often kept their conversations brief, on the edge of tense, even when they both were clearly happy with each other, pleased to be playing ball or talking books, enjoying a meal, whatever.

It was a book worried to the bone. An ivory artifact intricately gnawed and pawed and rubbed almost to transparency, but the marrow remained untouched. Intact. Perhaps this was his father's gift to him. Pops setting the table, providing the ingredients, inviting people to the feast, but leaving the final preparation of the meal for him.

Dear Dad. Just finished *Cattle Killing.* Congrats. A fine book. Look forward to talking about it with you soon. I could never sit down and write a formal critique of one of your novels, but sometimes I wish you could hear my thoughts as I read along. Interpolations, interpretations, digressions, footnotes. Factual queries, off-the-wall signifying and rewriting the text. I wish you could eavesdrop on some of that mess.

Sometimes your books seem to anticipate my wisecracks, misgivings, my groans and amens. We're rapping and capping tit for tat. Wish you could hear it. Maybe in a way you can. I certainly feel you there. A question, Father dear. If you play the dozens with your daddy, can you ever win.

You won't believe this. I discovered some unpublished letters during my stopover in London. My ticket gave me two days there and I spent them holed up in the British Museum's African archives. Found letters I wasn't searching for. A total, inexplicable fluke. The letters, I mean. I happened to find them stuck in a dusty box of dusty missionary correspondence and copied them, because letters from black Africans rarely survive from that period. It's just too bad I didn't discover them before you published your book. Remember now, I hadn't read your new book when I found the letters, wasn't even sure what your book was about, except you told me South Africa, the Xhosa cattle killing in it.

Anyway, for whatever reason the letters I found struck me, I made copies and now I find out the letters are a continuation of your book. A sort of happy ending, maybe. The whole business is spooky. Even if I'd unearthed them sooner, you wouldn't have been able to use the letters, because nobody would buy the spin they put on your story. The circle's too neat. Who would believe your narrator's brother, the one lost at sea off the Cape of Good Hope, or so the nameless narrator believed, would survive another fifty-some years in South Africa. Not only survive but keep a journal and write letters. The journal must be lost. At least, it's not in the same place I found the letters. References in the letters to a journal also describe it as missing in action. All I have is a few letters and fragments of letters in real bad shape. Letters to a brother a planet away, a brother the letter-writer hasn't glimpsed for decades. Outrageous, ain't it. Even the dates match up. Whether my letters and your story are actually, factually connected or not, a phenomenal coincidence. A relationship between brothers in the "real" world mirroring a relationship you made up for your book. Or vice versa. You call it.

The letters will speak for themselves. I intend to find a way to work them into my slave castle book so don't steal or quote without permission, sir. My lawyer and agent will be on your behind if you dare.

For your eyes only, then. I don't know if you based your book on real people, whatever *real* means. Point is the weird correspondence, either way. Truth stranger than fiction, Pop. I'm going to Xerox my copy of one letter, the only whole one, and send it now. Read and weep.

Love, D.J.

Brother, I have reached the verdant shores of Africa. Impossible adventures have delivered me here. I wept with joy and sorrow when my feet touched this African ground. I called out to you, our mother, our ancient fathers, to all I had lost and found on my journey.

Hollered your name, my brother, into the sweet, soaring African wind, because I need to tell you everything, everything . . .

I jumped ship. My mates were plotting to sell me to slavers. No black man is safe, even here. The country is in turmoil. Decades of war have left the African people landless, starving, dispirited. A prophecy has arisen and many Africans follow its mad reasoning. They are killing their cattle. This desperate measure is intended to drive away the whites, magically return the blacks to prosperity and power. But the effect of the wholesale destruction of their herds is exactly the opposite of what the Africans intend and the prophecy promised. Deeper misery settles over the land; the children are dying. The Africans are destroying themselves, doing to themselves what British guns and savagery could not accomplish.

I do not know how it will end, but I know my duty. I will pray for these noble, generous souls bewitched by a prophecy that steals them from themselves. I will struggle beside them as long as there is breath in my body.

This note, the others I intend to write, may never reach you, yet I am sure a time will come when we shall be together again.

Hold on, Your Brother